LIGHTS ALONG THE INTERSTATE

a novella by Adam Fike

For my loving Mother,
my darling Wife
and Our Ladies Of
The Seven Sorrows

TABLE OF CONTENTS:

INTRODUCTION

At the end of this story, tired from traveling but nowhere near home, Jack Eddy sits down outside a bus terminal and writes:

Humanity holds the strands of its history like straws in an outstretched fist. Long, short. Bent. Broken. None exactly as they were when the people who lived them thought to themselves: Well. Here I am. Right here. Right now.

A handful of these adventurers set off across a wide, gray ocean. On an errand all at once religious and political. The tale of woe that began when faith pointed a long, bony finger into the moral wilderness was their own living, breathing jeremiad. From the prophet Jeremiah, who talked about wicked people and their angry God. A mission to out-suffer the due punishment of all sinners. Shouldering thorny branches on humanity's behalf. Pain as progress. An empowering, giddy burden. These pilgrims brought this determination to what is now America.

It took no time for this group's war against the physics of human nature to fade from their sons' and daughters' sons and daughters. The aspect of inheritance on which old nations anchored themselves washed away. Along with the tradition of tradition, with tradition above all else.

In a place where fame is royalty, the upside is not hereditary.

Nevertheless, here children are the thrilling exception. Every single one. Their country correct. The only reasonable choice. A secular nation under God. A dysfunctional committee balancing freedom on the head of a pin. To lead. If not actually, then by stunning cultural example. An empowering, giddy burden.

In the feral opportunity of shimmering wilderness, brute force grows horns. Generations thrown down the barrels of war. Corruption finding all new cavities to entrench and rot. Each new wave beaten to submission and lining up to greet the next.

At no time else have so many accomplished so much so quickly. And along each step of the way, constituents enjoy their self-determined right to decide who created their world and why.

America names each person their own king. And each kingdom via their own best interest. Because you never know. This time next year, it could be you looking down from the top.

So, as every young, bright-eyed American gawks at their own bottomless potential, they participate in the nation's great test. This exceptional, modern jeremiad in an otherwise uncultured world.

But the exact, mathematical, measure of any civilization's progress, one brow-furrowed academic announced to members of the New York Historical Society as the nation slipped into civil war, is the precise degree to which modern minds prevail over their own accumulated wealth and aggression.

He meant, to know the place, meet the people.

ONE - ALBERT TAKES A WALK

The sun rises above a sprawling retirement home with complicated landscaping and its own tiny pond.

Behind a double-pane window on a middle floor, halfway between the senior condos and the medical wing, Albert snores peacefully. A Nurse nudges him.

Albert, she says. Time for your pills. Come on, now. Open up.

He doesn't budge.

No, it's not, he says.

Come on, Albert, she says. Open up.

Charlene, he says.

Albert, she says. Please.

No, Charlene, he says. Those pills are the ones to help me sleep. Blue with the stripe. You forgot to give them to me last night.

She dumps the pills into her hand.

Oh my, Albert, she says. You're right. I am so sorry. This overnight shift, with my kids and all, it's just killing me.

Perfectly fine, dear, he says. Just let an old man sleep.

Ok, she says. Ok. Sure, Albert. Sure.

She leaves. He rolls over and shuts his eyes hard. Too late. His bladder's up. So he's up.

Another day passes in all the usual ways. Morning recreation time. Lunch. Afternoon recreation time. The early news at four is now some gossip show. Otherwise, same as always. Always the same. Albert hangs around his room. Chair by the window. Reading books with history or maybe some cops or space. Never a big reader. Nothing else to do.

Out of the pages falls a picture of his lovely Wife on a vacation a lifetime ago. His bookmark. So happy. Smiling like the sun. Pointing out the distant ocean from a Florida motel parking lot, suitcases piled at her feet.

Albert tucks the book in a sweater pocket and tightens the suspenders he wore every Friday for all those years.

He looks around the little beige and lavender room. At the utility-grade carpet and rounded safety corners on the dorm furniture. Nothing else to bring beyond what's in his pockets. Except his cane and a jacket on a hook behind the door. That's all. He leaves it the way he found it in the color photo from the *Front Castle Retirement Home Guide to Senior Living*.

One of the Wives of one of his Sons, he doesn't know which one, got the glossy-paged Front Castle catalogue in the mail. Complete with the pale trees, shallow green lake and residents sitting stunned around a table playing cards. Some of them pretending to smile.

They all made believe it'd just arrived. The fees were already circled in the back. Albert didn't fight.

Doesn't this look nice, Dad, they asked.

Lovely afternoon, time for my walk, Albert chimes, slipping past the Nurse's Station at the end of his hall.

Okey-dokey, a different Nurse mumbles into a soda, flipping through a magazine, never looking up.

Lovely, Albert chuckles, turning down the stairs.

Roast beef tonight, Artie, shouts the new Senior Living Manager in a pastel blazer, shuffling day-old flowers in a vase near the dining room door. Everybody's favorite!

Sounds terrific, Albert smiles.

This isn't the same Senior Living Manager from that first issue of the Guide. Or the one they met on move-in day, when his kids snuck off to speak privately so he could try out his new room.

Isn't this great, Dad, they asked.

But whichever brand new Manager always wore the same plastic corsage with the corporate logo. And Albert doesn't know her name either, so he feels they part on an even footing.

Down near the lake, a few of his hallmates sit at a patio table sinking unevenly into the grass, playing cards.

Two were in this year's Guide, in a picture along with Albert in the pool, clutching blue foam kickboards. The caption read: *Mel, Albert and Don love their time in our fully heated Olympic-size pool!*

Don was recovering from a stroke, and the photographer kept turning him in the water to get the side that still grinned. He's the only one smiling.

Hey Dad, big news, his Sons told him over the phone. You made the Guide!

Boys, I'm in the wind, Albert says between long shuffles, nodding mostly to Mel, who's the only one that can really hear him.

How's that, Mel asks.

Mum's the word Albert says and pats Don's shoulder.

They don't know who they're playing with, Albert, Don says.

They certainly don't, Albert chuckles. Cover for me, Mel, for whatever time you can.

Sure, sure, good luck, Mel says, never taking his eyes off the game.

Albert follows the path around the lake with a pocketful of dinner rolls. Ducks gather at his ankles. Squirrels track him from the trees. Albert checks his watch against the clock tower on the Front Castle Chapel/Synagogue/Conference Center. Then crumbles the always-stale rolls in a wide circle as the birds happily gather. He takes a last look at the tidy cluster of faceless buildings and passes quickly into the trees.

Meeting a cab down the road, Albert hands the guy a

twenty for his effort and thanks him for waiting.

Where to, the Cab Driver asks.

Bus depot in town, please, Albert says.

You from that place up the road, the Cab Driver asks.

Ah, yeah, Albert says. Guess so.

Isn't that like a hospital or something, the Cab Driver asks.

Albert fires off the disarming smile of somebody too far along to quit now, as well as a few more bills.

Don't worry, he says. I'm not sick. Just old.

Doors slam and they're off.

Right then, the air hangs heavy inside the nearest bus station break room. In a rumpled uniform and crooked hat, a brand new Bus Driver patiently waits for a reaction.

Outside, groaning metal pachyderms come and go. Inside, Passengers wander around and wonder what's next.

Beyond the snack bar and lockers, down a long arrow of buzzing lights, George stares back across the orange Formica table between them. Collecting his thoughts. Scratching his jaw through a long sideburn. Stalling.

Leaning back in his chair, thick arms re-crossing a faded T-shirt, George says, I mean, I don't rightly know.

The Bus Driver smiles and nods.

Now, George, he says. I want you to just relax and tell me the truth. Wouldn't you, if you were me?

The small room falls quiet again. George studies the vending machine. A minute clicks away on a heavy metal clock on a shelf in the corner, next to the time cards.

If I were you, George says. Me?

Yes, the Bus Driver says. Pretend.

But how would that work, George asks. Can you really just . . .

The Bus Driver claps his hands and straightens his hat.

Precisely, he says. No idea. So we're going to find out

together.

The Bus Driver heads for the door. George knocks his chair over backwards on the way to his feet.

For how long, George asks.

Have a little faith, alright, the Bus Driver says.

George just stares at him.

Do you know baseball, George, the Bus Driver asks. Do you like baseball?

Sure, he says.

Yeah, the Bus Driver says. So take a pitcher, for instance. They throw the ball out there with some control. But after they let it go, all they can do is stand around like everybody else. They fling it out there. They do their best. But after that, it's all about . . .

The Bus Driver stares down at his reflection in a cup of cold coffee leaving a ring on the flimsy table.

. . . balance, he says. And wind. And gravity. And spin. Lots and lots of spin.

George nods, resetting his chair.

You're the boss, he says.

Not even a little, the Bus Driver says. How's the diner?

Still there, last time I checked, George says.

And the kids, the Bus Driver asks. How're they doing?

So far so good, George says. I like them.

There's a lot to like, says the Bus Driver, stepping out the break room door.

At the end of the fluorescent hallway, on his way into the main terminal, the Bus Driver picks up a clipboard with his identification number written large in marker across the top.

Flipping pages, he emerges from behind the ticket counter and stops next to Albert, sitting in a folding chair with his cane propped against it.

Evening, Albert says.

Evening, the Bus Driver says.

Storms brewing, Albert says. Should find us before long.

Premonition, the Bus Driver asks.

Weather Channel, Albert says, waving his cane at a dingy monitor mounted on a yellowed wall above the wooden benches full of travelers who stare, sleep or don't, beneath the looping video.

The Bus Driver pulls a set of keys from his pocket and turns towards a side door.

Throughout the huge terminal, dust pumps from filthy, ancient ducts. The air holds a tinge the Bus Driver can taste. He steps outside.

Outside is humid. Muggy. But crystal clear. Huge clouds licking the ground in the distance shove a breeze past his face that whistles in his ears. The Bus Driver smiles.

Climbing onto his bus, he stares down at the dials and switches, studying each one like a new toy. He turns the key. Pumps the pedal. The engine chugs, then hums.

After a muffled announcement inside the terminal, Albert leads a weary line toward the bus door. The Bus Driver meets each rider quietly with his eyes. They find vinyl seats along the aisle, spreading out in their best impersonal, broken pattern.

Lifting the microphone from a hook over his head, the Bus Driver begins to announce their various destinations. He stops and hangs it back up. They know where they're going.

He pops free the air brake. Easing the clutch, the Bus Driver carefully grits his teeth. The bus jerks twice but rolls and picks up speed across the parking lot. They pass blocks of dark homes and stores, cross railroad tracks and for miles see nothing but night.

Soon, the bus rocks smoothly as the Passengers each fall into uncomfortable, twisted, vertical sleep.

TWO - SUCH A PRETTY HEART

Long asphalt ribbons drag headlights home, through unlit mountain forests scattered with deer eyes, blinking and concerned.

House windows flashing with television screens form streamlets flowing into gas stations and fast-food signs puddling among cloverleafs and off-ramps.

Neon shouts *open* across the vacant Paradise Diner parking lot, nearly alone on a hushed stretch of road. Inside, a rumpled Accountant teeters on the edge of embezzlement.

Red-top stools flank a long, coffee-smudged counter. Pies under thick glass. Tubes buzz and flicker from window to window and back.

He spreads a stack of company books, clammy and uncertain. Hesitates. Then opens them, pen leaking in his shirt pocket. He reaches for it and twitches with frustration.

Waving the dripping plastic tube, he looks to a portly Waitress hovering behind the cash register. Her name tag says Irene. Irene ignores him.

He wraps the pen in a napkin and shoves it back into his pocket.

Excuse me, he coughs across the otherwise empty room.

Irene chews her gum and stares into a paperback. A barely clad couple grapple on the cover.

Ma'am, he coughs.

Irene ignores him.

Could you put down your smutty little book a minute and bring me some coffee, he grumbles. Please?

Historical book, Irene corrects him without looking up.

What, he asks.

Charging him, elbows flying, Irene throws the paperback down on the counter.

It's historical, she says, thumping the book cover with a stubby finger.

What, he asks again, still confused.

Right there, she says. See the castle? Historical!

He silently watches her charge into the kitchen. Then the Accountant stiffens. Suddenly he's not alone. He's flanked by two burly figures eating pie. The big one wears biker's leather, the little one wears sailor's wool.

Dilly of a pickle, friend, says the Big Demon, pawing and spreading the papers across the counter.

Excuse me, the Accountant nearly squeals. I'm sorry?

The Accountant is sweating.

That's no sort of attitude, the Little Demon chuckles, sloshing what's left of the Accountant's coffee to his mouth. How much are we talking about?

He sets the cup down on the counter. A dark smoke ring circles the edges.

Not much, not even six figures, the Big Demon says.

You know, the jerk you work for blows more company money than that twice a year on his stupid boat, the Little Demon says. Don't even get started thinking about that. Right out of the company till. That and all the cars. The vacation house. Ski trips. Condo in the islands. Company property. For clients only and closing big deals. But who's got the keys? Without the common decency to throw a holiday party. That's the funny thing about numbers. An accountant's creation.

I hate that damn boat, the Accountant says.

Don't blame you, the Big Demon says. But you'll file it under miscellaneous with the rest. And put it out of your mind. That's the job. Not the actual work. Processing the full accounts of one of the largest operations of its kind in the whole damn country. It's dealing with the nonsense. The part with no fairness or rhyme or reason. Or merit. That's the job.

Check please, the Accountant squeaks to no one.

Irene's still gone, thudding around in the kitchen. The Demons settle in close.

After all, the Little Demon says. Who's to say what numbers are on the wall at the end of the month? Who really writes all those checks? Shifts it all around and softens those hard edges? Can't trust the computer. Everybody knows that. That thing thinks up new mistakes every day. Sure. In that sea of numbers? It's simple. If you keep track. Keep it small. Quiet. Like magic.

How could, the Accountant sputters. Who told . . . Who . . .

Their skin is scaly. Their hair greasy. Their eyes the wrong shade of blue.

What they owe you is such a tiny hunk to break off, the Big Demon says. It's not even about the dollars.

No, it's about respect, the Little Demon says. And a new brick patio. Instead of that crooked, uneven thing you have out there now.

Well, sure, that, the Big Demon says. And a new car. The V8 this time.

Straight teeth for the kid, the Little Demon says. It's only right. And fair, for what?

Twenty-five years' service, the Big Demon says. Sixty hours a week, and what's that title? Associate Vice President? Hashtag, sad. But who's to say what's fair?

Their eyes meet in the stainless steel behind the counter.

Me, the Accountant says.

The Demons grin.

Irene marches through the kitchen door.

Hey, no smoking, she thunders.

Not smoking, honey, the Big Demon says. Just breathing.

Irene rolls her eyes and shoves her way back into the kitchen.

Outside, trees bend to the ground. Thick rain splatters windows. Drums the roof.

The diner door sweeps open and a complete lack of sound gushes in. The opposite of noise circles the stools. Twirls beneath table tops. Ear-splittingly empty.

The Big Demon and the Little Demon leap to disheveled attention. The Accountant remains working, oblivious.

The Devil, a long way from a nap or shower, steps into the diner, perfectly dry and dressed for after a dinner party. As the door closes, a bell begins mid-cry and finishes.

In the far corner of the diner, Jesus emerges from the men's room, tucking a handkerchief into his coat pocket.

Hello, darling, Satan says.

Sit down, says Jesus. I'm busy.

Together they slide into a booth. Irene plants herself again behind the counter, unaware of the rank of her company.

Satan whirls on the Little Demon and the Big Demon, slouching awkwardly nearby.

Beat it, he hisses, mostly to amuse himself.

The Demons gratefully flee.

It's been so long since we really talked, Satan says.

What do you want, Jesus asks.

Oh, right, Satan says. I quit.

Quit, Jesus asks.

You heard me, junior, Satan says. I'm leaving the act. You're on your own.

I have no idea what you're talking about, Jesus says.

The Devil raises his hand. Irene approaches wearing a button: *Angels Sing the Lord's Praises*.

Hello, sweetheart, how are you this evening, Satan asks.

Just fine, she says, gnawing a worn pen. Yourself?

Wicked, Satan says. May I ask you a question?

Sure, she says. Shoot.

Have you accepted Jesus Christ as your personal savior, he asks.

Jesus groans.

Well, of course, she says.

Yes, of course, Satan says. But will you help my derelict friend here with why, exactly?

She blushes, doodling on a menu.

Uhm, well, to keep the Devil out, she says.

Out, Satan asks.

Of my heart, she says.

Such a pretty girl, Satan says. With such a pretty heart.

She giggles, flopping down their menus, swaying from the table. Her phone number scratched across the corner of the daily specials. Circled with a heart.

Jesus stands.

So tell me, how does the Devil quit, he asks.

Damned if I know, Satan says, stepping closer and smiling. Well, that's it. I could dance all night, but I have places to be. Over and out.

He passes through the diner door.

Jesus sits and looks over the menu.

Fine with me, he says. Excuse me? That coffee hot?

Rain pelts the parking lot. Satan laughs beneath the streetlights and rises into the night.

The same rain falls sharply against an apartment window not even a mile away. A gently sleeping girl curls a giant cat in her arms.

Satan flutters in, crouching on the sill. Then he slides in beside her.

They met in a roadside bar. He sat in a Western-theme booth. Wagon wheels and fringe. Dirty glasses on the table. Dirty thoughts in the air. Bored. Toying with the idea of starting a fire.

Then there she stood. Through the smoke and idle shouting. Taking shape, little by little.

She conned her way across the room. Picking. Coaxing. Teasing. Searching. Not finding what she rummaged for.

Then she spotted him. The perfect center point of the all the dark urges colliding around her. A current tumbling past and through him. A pivot she saw, somehow. Evident. Vibrant. Delicious.

His identity? No. His gravity? Absolutely.

She approaches. He smiles. She tingles. He sees it.

So the Devil fell a second time. Then very sweetly, she stole his watch.

The Girl rolls over in bed and smiles.

Hey there, she says.

And he so loved this girl that he gave up his horns to be the Devil no more.

THREE - A CLEAN SLATE

A heavy morning crowd fills the booths and counters of the Paradise Diner. A wiry, bright-eyed Boy, twenty going on fifty, throws eggs at a busy grill, running the whole show.

Order up, he yells.

A bashful Cook, twice his age, appears at the back door.

Sorry, he says.

There you are, The Boy says. The hell you been?

Slept through my alarm again, he says.

The Boy unties his apron and throws it at the Cook.

I'm buying you a new clock, he says. A loud, angry clock. Got it?

Yeah, the Cook says. Sorry.

The back door clangs open. A muscular man in a cloth jacket, stitched with George above the pocket, lugs in a hand truck piled with boxes. His face shows more than a fight or two, along with the worry from his conversation with the Bus Driver at the depot.

Who could possibly eat this much mustard, George asks.

Hey, I'll give you a hand, The Boy says, following him outside.

A delivery truck sits out front. George tosses The Boy boxes from the back.

Beautiful day, The Boy chimes.

You say so, George says.

Ever feel like some days just anything can happen, The Boy asks.

George shrugs.

Watch what you wish for, he says.

They work on for a long moment.

How's my Uncle, The Boy asks.

Fine, George says. Busy. Sends his best.

Doesn't come around much, The Boy says.

That's what I'm here for, George says. Make sure you keep the place standing.

They both laugh for different reasons.

Two states away, the rising sunlight burns off morning fog amid the ripening leaves of a rotting suburb.

The little girl who lives where the main road parts finishes putting away her toys. This is Morgan. Her letters, notes and journal lay in ashes at the bottom of her Father's wood stove. The makeup her aunts bought her fit in a cardboard box she slides under her bed.

Sitting in the center of the bed, her eyes drift over a collection of pictures her Father hung throughout the house over the years – a consecutive series of department store family portraits.

As they progress, her Mother fades. Sicker and sicker. Until she's gone. Then a new woman in her place. Smiling. Uncomfortable. Increasingly evident in astoundingly floral prints. Morgan carefully piles them into milk crates stacked in her closet. Sharp bruises from a tight, manicured grip run up and down her arms.

The crates below are books and toys. Her stuffed animals on the very bottom. Roller skates just above that. A plastic bag of orphaned dice and board game pieces. A hand me-down softball glove. A tangle of jump ropes and chalk. The yearbooks. Middle school, freshman year, distracted class portraits with cloudy backgrounds. A framed certificate of perfect attendance cracks from the weight.

Digging through the top box she finds a last, smaller, frame. Morgan slips the backing off and slides the picture free. Without a glance, she tears the photograph of herself and her Mother in two. Crumpling and throwing her part aside, she closes the doors.

In a sudden, swift move, she tugs down cheerful matching curtains, folds them neatly and shoves them under the bed.

With the picture of her Mother in her back pocket, she quietly slides out onto the carport roof.

Across the street, Mary, dressed all in blue, watches Morgan hang from the drain spout and fall lightly onto the grass.

Don't go, she says. The words barely escape her throat.

This time of year, rain pours steadily over the town. But right now, a patch of sun shines on the rolled shoulders of the rumpled Bus Driver's uniform, planted on a bench beside an overgrown pine.

Shimmering green carpet rolls before him. The Bus Driver digs into a paper bag for his lunch. He waits.

The bus fills with gas at a minimart a few blocks away. The Passengers use the bathroom, look at magazines, and stretch their legs.

This park is where a handful of streets meet at the outskirts of a town barely breathing on its own. Trees set close together press out a ring of empty storefronts. In a place where most open land is paved, filthy and vacant, the people spared this slice of forest from progress.

Grim morning traffic circles the park on the way to factories on one side of the county or industrial parks and cubicle farms on the other. And as each car passes a narrow point on the north side, commuters glance up at a statue's broad shoulders.

The worn plaque at her feet says Mother Nature. She is tall, with broad shoulders and flowing stone robes. One long, outstretched hand points intently into the thick foliage and directly at the bench where the Bus Driver stopped to eat his lunch. Her eyes scan the leaves. Guarding them. Fastening them there. Her face set with deep concentration.

The Bus Driver unwraps a tuna fish sandwich from the gas station deli and balances it on his knee. He unscrews the cap of a small thermos. Clouds continue to shift politely above him. He sits beneath the only patch of blue sky.

Morgan reaches the end of the block she grew up on.

Stop, that's the wrong way, Mary says.

Morgan doesn't know she's there.

Mary watched Morgan fade away after her Mother was gone. Staring out the window. Seeing just the glass.

Morgan gave up slowly, at first. Then faster all the time. Until sad just meant tired and sleep meant forget.

Reaching the hill leading down into the park, Morgan stops. Mary catches her breath.

The streets are quiet and cold. Doors shut. Commuters gone. Rows of small houses shove porches into tiny lots. Short driveways. Small hedges.

Go home, Mary says to Morgan, unheard. Go home.

Where she parts the trees, Morgan faces the statue.

Taking a bite of his sandwich, the Bus Driver watches, chewing. Morgan crosses the grass. Her shoes fall away. She kicks at the dark, soft blades, skipping. And stops at the statue's feet.

Squinting up at the stone woman's face, Morgan moves to put the outstretched arm between herself and the sun. There Morgan stands for a long, long time.

The Bus Driver and Mary wait. He chews his sandwich. She kneads her palms.

Over the years, this statue caused continual distress for the town council. Digging their toes into the folds of the stone woman's robes, the children could climb to her shoulders. They all did it once, or tried. It meant being one of the big kids. But the monument also came at moderate expense and to change it was out of the question.

Walking behind the stone woman, Morgan reaches up to find hand holds nearest her height. In a few quick moves, she is onto the statue's back. A few more and she perches on the shoulder, balancing precariously at first, then resting in the crook of the arm.

The Bus Driver finishes his sandwich, folding the butcher paper neatly. His eyes stare into the statue's. Neither blinks.

Slowly, Morgan slides a belt from the waist of her cut-off jeans. This is her Father's belt, thick and heavy.

Fishing into her pocket, she touches a thin bolt and nut she found a long time ago in the corner of the garage. She unscrews them.

It takes a while to punch a hole through the belt, using the end of the bolt carefully sharpened with a file. First sliding the end through the buckle, she brings it around the woman's forearm, fastening the end to its middle like a loose armband. Then she fastens the nut and bolt, forming another loop.

Mary turns her back to the statue and Morgan, staring intently at the Bus Driver sitting on the bench. He gazes calmly, miserably, into her eyes.

With the first loop fastened to the arm, the inside of the other now rests warmly against the back of Morgan's thin neck. She takes a look around. No one in sight. And with no hesitation, turns and swings free of the stone shoulder.

Sinking to her knees, Mary drives her face into the wet grass and holds it there. She sobs for a while but doesn't have much of that left in her. Mary raises her face again to the statue and rises to her feet. Steadying, she pulls a long blade of grass from her hair.

Morgan hangs motionless now.

I'm sorry, the Bus Driver says.

Mary turns to face him.

Are you, she asks.

Right then, morning finds a phone ringing in a spotless,

though aging townhouse on a once-proud, but now downwardly mobile street.

The ornate phone rings sharply, rattling a highly polished end table in a superbly arranged parlor room. It rings again.

A gaunt man with a pencil-thin mustache paces nearby, watching it ring. A red rose pinned to the lapel of his jet-black suit, his attention does not waiver from the phone. He seems to enjoy the distraction.

A small and stately local Reverend appears at the door. She wipes her hands on an apron, protecting a neat, purple outfit.

Don't just stand there watching it ring, she says. You may come and get me.

Seventeen rings, he says. Must be important. You know, lots of people have hearing aids these days. We'll buy a cute hat to cover your ears.

Hush, she says.

The phone rings again.

Eighteen, he says.

The Reverend picks up the heavy receiver. An agitated series of harrumphs pour from the line.

Yes, she says. Yes, I apologize for that. But I did answer. We're speaking right now. Yes. Of course. Well, I do not prefer the term supernatural. No. Well, perfectly natural, I suppose. Correct. Yes, it's all in your letter. Yes, that as well. Very good. Alright, see you then.

The Reverend gently hangs up the phone.

Time to go, she says.

In the apartment not far from the diner, sunlight rising into his eyes, Satan yawns. Arching against the mattress, he stretches every way at once. Then, with a pleasant moan, he falls back asleep.

Perched on the end table next to the bed, the large cat

peers down at him. An ink-covered notepad hangs over the edge. The cat carefully cleans behind its ears.

From the long, flat rooftop a few stories above, Jesus watches The Girl slip out of the building with quick steps, a bag over her shoulder.

Satan sits up and startles the cat. It bolts beneath the bed, skidding on the notepad, which follows the cat to the floor. Rubbing his eyes, he notices writing across the pad and reaches for it. Jolting as his mind focuses, he leaps from the bed.

Down the street, The Girl holds a palm against the growing sun. The Boy from the diner leans against a wall, waiting. She bounds toward him, grabbing his hand.

Hi, baby, she says.

Jesus looks down from the roof and checks his watch.

The Boy fishes in his pocket for keys as they climb into a beat-up green car parked on the corner. She throws out her arms and kisses him.

So, he says.

So, I'm all yours, she says.

Good, he says, turning the key. Good.

Jesus doesn't wait long. A door bursts open and Satan explodes onto the roof, eyes sweeping the streets below. Then he spots Jesus standing at the roof's far corner. Curses echoes off the sky.

Now, now, Jesus says.

Satan rushes him, his fist clenching the piece of paper.

What did you do, he demands.

Not a thing, Jesus shrugs.

Satan unravels the paper and waves it in his face.

This is my new life now, I'm sorry, he reads. What did you do?

Me, Jesus asks sincerely.

Yeah, Satan says.

Not a thing, Jesus says.

Funny boy, Satan says. Always with the funny jokes.

The Boy's car chatters down a road leading out of town, passing a sign for a local community college.

The Girl fiddles with the radio dial and pulls a stack of application papers from her bag.

You want help with that essay later tonight, he asks. After work?

Thought you'd never ask, she says.

The Boy grins.

Satan stomps in a circle.

I'll kill him, he says.

You won't touch him, Jesus says.

And why is that, Satan asks.

Because I like him, Jesus says. And he's not even halfway up your list of problems.

You just say things like that to agitate me, Satan mutters as he steps off the roof edge.

He touches down amid the bustle of commuters bleeding from the buildings into their day. Jesus lands close behind.

And where are we off to, Jesus asks.

Satan shoulders his way through the morning crowd, Jesus in his wake. The commuters are aware of them, with no idea who they are.

Hungry, Satan says. Thinking about a little meddling bastard for breakfast.

Jesus blocks his path with a grin. Satan moves one way, then the other. Jesus matches him left and right.

Oh, Satan says. Now? Really?

Satan shoves Jesus aside. Jesus follows, nearly skipping.

Jesus Christ, Satan says. Will you please just leave me alone?

See, it's funny when you say it that way, Jesus says.

Satan stops and turns, slapping a cup of coffee from a passing Commuter's hand.

Hey, he yells.

Satan snarls as the coffee-soaked Commuter retreats.

You know, I never liked you, Satan says. Big fake.

Jesus smiles, I've done my share.

Satan continues on, Jesus a step behind.

Stop following me, Satan growls.

They reach a street corner amid a crowd of Grade Schoolers stopped by a Crossing Guard. Satan pushes past the Guard into the street, narrowly slipping by speeding cars, horns blaring.

Jesus waits at the curb.

Guess you can hear about it like everybody else, he says. I'm the dummy for wasting my time with you.

Satan stops.

What, he groans.

Now it's Jesus's turn to be distracted. By the pretty morning around them. The deep sky and friendly people.

Extending a wooden sign, the Crossing Guard walks to the middle of the street. Cars stop. The children begin to cross.

Satan balls his fists.

Alright, he says. About what?

Jesus's attention is on the children around him. He guides them into the street, showing off a little. Satan swipes the stop sign from the Crossing Guard's hands and flings it at Jesus. The wooden sign smacks Jesus in the chest. He catches it hard. It hurts.

You heard me, Satan says. I'll bite.

Jesus's eyes narrow as he charges past him, handing the sign to the dismayed Crossing Guard.

Piss off, he says.

Hey, not in front of the kids, Satan says.

Jesus hits the curb and charges on, turning down an alleyway between buildings.

Now Satan follows him.

Come on, he says. Fair's fair.

Jesus turns back. He yanks a glass vial from his pocket.

You know what this is, he asks.

Satan laughs.

You should have said you were holding, he says.

Jesus turns down a set of filthy stairs leading to basement apartments. He shoves open a splattered door. Satan follows him along a dank hallway.

Pride in a bottle, Jesus says. Quick burst of everything's right with the world.

Jesus turns a corner and kicks his way into an apartment. Dim light trickles in through boarded-up windows.

The room is mostly empty except for trash and a layer of filth. Sprays of blood on the walls. In the middle is a thin, sickly Junkie nodding out in a hard, wooden chair. A spoon on the floor beside him. Needle dangling from his arm.

Bad medicine, says Satan, leaning against the door frame. But what are we talking about?

Jesus steps behind the Junkie.

Another chance, he says.

Trees whip past the windows as The Girl and Boy from the Paradise Diner happily drive on, stealing glances at each other and smiling. She wraps her fingers around his hand on the gear shift.

Jesus holds the small vial to the one beam of sunlight penetrating the grimy apartment. It twinkles.

A couple of kids, he says. A choice. A temptation . . . A warning. An outcome.

I read the book, Satan says.

They both just say no and we'll do it all over again, Jesus says. The right way. Blank slate. Right down to the timbers. Like you always wanted. Leave them alone. You and me, the rest, we'll stay completely out of it this time. We'll see how they do on their own for once. No push. No pull. No screwing around.

You can't be serious, Satan says.

A new start, Jesus says. A clean slate.

The cities, culture, Satan says. The people. Their lives. Gone?

What do you care, Jesus asks. You quit. Right?

Correct, Satan says and turns to leave. Got my own problems.

I'll say, Jesus says.

The green car pulls up to the curb in front of administrative offices for the small community college.

Wish me luck, she says.

You don't need it, he says.

She slides into his lap and smiles.

I like you a lot, she says.

Not her, Satan says, stunned. Anybody but her.

This all started long before you met her, Jesus says.

I don't put a lot of stock in coincidence, Satan says.

Believe whatever you want, Jesus says. I'm wrong. They give in. We just keep going. Who knows, maybe you'll win her back someday. But I'm betting they both want to be good. I'm still betting they all want to be good.

Jesus sets his hands on the nodding Junkie's shoulders. The Junkie jerks awake, startled, panicked, and confused.

The Devil grins.

I'll take that bet, he says.

FOUR - JOHNNY AND GOLIATH

As the sun sets, the rain picks up. An angry glass cube sits frozen to a concrete slab beside the highway, twitching in a puddle of light. Truckers rumble past, battering the wind, rattling the tiny building out of place among the trees.

A man shaped like a five-and-a-half-foot fireplug in a heavy gray coat pushes through the doors. He drops a duffel bag to the concrete, rubs his hands together and scratches an ear. Pulling off a scarf, he finds a bench in the center of the room, next to a kid from a nearby college, piled with books and bags.

The kid stares absently at a Classmate on the other bench, getting pawed at through her clothes by a giant fella with a lot of rings and long hair. Fog grows on the glass around them.

The kid sighs. The man clears his throat.

What time's it there, pal, he asks.

Twenty 'till, the kid says.

You know them, he asks.

We go to school up the road, the kid says. They gave me a ride.

A metallic moan behind them sends a low vibration through the building. Headlights flash the windows. A sharp shriek. The rumble stops. They all look up to see the side of a bus.

She puts both hands on the big lug and pushes. He stands, well over six-nine. Together, they gather her things.

Goodbye, Johnny, have a real nice break, she says, throwing a bag over her shoulder. See you when we get back.

Johnny waves. The two stay locked together, steam rising all around them, the whole way to the bus steps.

She finds a window seat and presses her face against the glass. At his height, they are nearly eye to eye. The giant touches the window as the bus rolls away. When it's gone, he pulls keys from his pocket, climbs into a tiny tin-can pickup and disappears into the night.

Irv, the man says.

John, the guy says. Johnny. That was her new friend. See, I thought we were almost dating. Or something. But, turns out, that's the new friend she was talking about, who could give us a ride over here. Don't worry, I had a tarp in the back. And his name is Goliath. His real name. Like, they knew that was going to happen when he was a baby.

No kidding, Irv says.

Nope, Johnny says. No kidding.

Good luck with that, Johnny, Irv says.

The building shakes again as their bus appears through the rain. Johnny and Irv gather their things and head for the door.

Stepping into the gleaming column of water blocking their way to the bus, they both glance over at the same time to see the Reverend standing alone in the crook of wall near the door. It's a sharp, dark corner where the building's overhang meets a gun-gray metal strut.

The Reverend huddles beneath a small, round, purple umbrella, through rain swirling in giant globs.

They part to let her up the bus steps, but she stops near the top. Waiting there with a tattered bible tucked under her arm, she stares sternly out the door as they pass the Bus Driver their tickets. As he pulls shut the door, she puts a hand on his shoulder.

Wait, please, she says.

The Bus Driver stops.

Ma'am, he says.

Hold the door, she says. Please.

He waits. She glares into the rain.

The pale man in his long, black suit steps onto the bus, perfectly dry.

Alright, Reverend, alright, he says. All I'm saying is we could have rented a car on a night like this.

She turns. He follows her down the aisle, the back of his suit coat slit to the collar. The Bus Driver smiles as he closes the door. The bus sighs out onto the highway and deep into the night.

Thirty miles from the Paradise Diner, the rain passes. The sky grows clear. The Passengers doze and the Bus Driver takes on a long stare.

A deer's steps slow in the perfect silence of complete night. Headlights. Tiny glinting eyes. The Bus Driver's hands lock at the wheel. The body collapses into the charging front bumper. Then it's over. The bus never blinks.

By a quarter-to-three, Johnny and Irv eat pie at the counter of the Paradise Diner, sandwiched into an uncomfortable silence by a growing argument between Jack Eddy and a fat traveling Salesman.

The Reverend sips coffee a few booths away.

Albert sits upright, snoring on the bus.

Behind the counter, Irene shakes huge, plastic, coffee-ground bags in each hand. She pours the brown powder into an industrial-size coffee machine.

Dusting her hands on her dustier apron, she ducks into the kitchen, passing the grill, thick in the corners with gristle, then the cooler. She pushes sideways into a dark space behind the giant refrigerator, swinging open a thin wooden door and stepping into the storeroom.

Squatting on a plastic pickle barrel, The Girl, who stole the Devil's heart, reaches up at her with a joint.

The Boy leans in the corner.

Hey, anything burning out there, he asks.

Didn't look, Irene says. Those ugly guys at the counter need something.

What, The Girl asks.

I don't know, Irene says. They just have that look.

You could've asked when you walked by, says The Girl, in a matching waitress uniform.

The counter is all yours, Irene says.

Jack Eddy slides the ketchup along the diner counter to Irv, who knocks it out onto eggs.

The Salesman dives back into his rhubarb pie, pudgy fingers wrapping his fork, chewing roundly. The sides of his thin tan suit nearly pushing Irv into the aisle.

They are talking about The Girl. She has that, what-the-hell-are-you-doing-here look, they all agree.

She, for instance, would take a guy like you and break him up for parts, Eddy says. And that, pal, is just a fact.

But, what a way to go, the fat man says.

The diner's the kind that's wheeled in and clamped onto a slab. Encased in thick glass and aluminum. A memorial to itself. Slumping from the corners. Past due slipping quietly off the road into a nearby gully for a nap.

The two-lane road out front curves into darkness both ways. A filling station on the other side yawns next to a sleepy church. The bus waits quietly at the only pump.

Leaning between the door and the blood-smudged bumper, the Bus Driver's jaw hurts from clenching.

Mary steps to the edge of the half ring of light.

How's that feel, she asks.

How's what feel, he sighs.

There are tears in her eyes.

An accident, she says. Or at least, something horrible you didn't mean. A terrible moment. Out of nowhere. Hurts.

You're angry, he says.

I'm tired, she says.

What would you like me to do, he asks. Tell me.

Something, she says.

That's not fair, he says.

Isn't it, she asks.

The Bus Driver plants his hands on his knees.

These things happen, he says.

Across the road in the diner, his Passengers mill about, eating or heading for the bathroom.

Bending over the bloody bumper, he touches the metal and rubs the color between his fingers. Then he turns toward the rear of the bus. She follows.

I want an explanation, she says.

What more can I tell you, he asks.

Not for me, she says.

On the far side of the asphalt, Morgan, with her thick brown belt around her waist, stands in the shadows. She tugs a long hair from her eyes and studies them both.

Well, Mary asks.

The Bus Driver passes his palm across his forehead, down his chin and then toward Morgan, waving her over.

Hesitating slightly, Morgan crosses the road.

Hello, the Bus Driver says.

Hi, Morgan says.

Tell you what, let's take a walk, he says.

Pump still hooked to the bus, the Bus Driver leads them away toward the sagging church.

Morgan and Mary follow him inside. A deep red carpet stretches past a handful of dusty pews. Banks of candles light the corners.

You know, birds don't train squirrels to guard their nests, the Bus Driver says. Trees don't go to college. Alligators have no hobbies. A hippopotamus never paved anything. The truth about things is never exhausting for them.

The Bus Driver turns and leads them up some back steps. Together, they slide into a pew amid the shadows of the balcony.

There was this moment thousands and thousands of years ago, he says. The world wasn't alive like it is now. Only this one perfect spot. One happy little valley. Full of these very happy people. Until the seas shifted and filled their valley. They ran and screamed. Blamed each other. Then all together they cried out. And there I was.

What did you do, Morgan asks.

Not a thing, the Bus Driver says. At first. Then too much. I feel bad. It's not easy being the animal that knows it's going to die. You need to surrender to something. To forgive yourselves. To digest what's going to happen. It's a powerful thing. So you create what you need. That's the best part of people, most of the time. Same as everything else you build. It all works great until you fight over it.

Below them, the door opens and Albert shuffles in, heading toward a pew up front.

That's Albert, the Bus Driver says. Every night, every morning and sometimes at lunch, he gets down on his knees and he prays. And when his eyes close at night, his mind rests. He falls asleep grinning. Forgetting right then that someday he won't open those eyes. And he sleeps this wonderful sleep. Remarkable thing. Sleep.

Inside the diner, beneath the swinging, naked storeroom lightbulb, Irene picks dully at an old tub of macaroni salad with long, pressed-on nails.

Look, Irene, I need to take off early, The Boy says. You got to run the grill.

Fine, she says. But we split tips. Not filling up my pores with grease all night for nothing.

Sorry, The Girl says. I need you to cover for me.

Run that past me again, Irene snorts.

You heard me, The Girl says. I worked for you all day Thursday. You can sure as hell close one time on your own.

Nobody else is coming in here tonight, The Boy says.

Take a nap if you want to.

Irene knows he's right and snorts.

Fine, abandon me here, she says.

The Boy grins as he pushes past her. Catching a mop handle stuck in a wheeled bucket, he shoves his way out the door.

In the church balcony, Morgan leans forward and crosses her arms on the railing. She watches the candle shadows shooting down the pews.

The Bus Driver seats himself at an organ at the far end of the balcony. The keys don't play.

And that brings us to you, he says. They didn't get it.

Not really, Morgan says.

They were trying, he says.

I know, she says. I'm sorry.

I should hope so, he says. Such an ugly waste.

Below them, the kneeler in Albert's pew snaps back into place. He struggles to stand. Crossing himself, he makes his way out the door.

So here's the thing, the Bus Driver says. The way this works is, now you owe me. Or really, them. So, I've got a couple things for you to take care of. It's not going to be fun.

One by one, The Girl fills the coffee cups along the counter. The men watch, mumbling thanks.

Welcome, boys, she says, sorting out their checks.

What I'm talking about, it's like America, says the Salesman, watching The Girl disappear into the kitchen.

Nobody bites. Irv sighs.

What's like America, he asks.

Change, the Salesman says. Faster cars. Faster food. Faster people. Skirts on a woman look good. Little miniskirts look better. Progress. Change. Change means grab a girl like that. Because by the time she's done with you, you're done with her and on to someone even better. It's the American way. If it's here too long, it's evil.

A big, meaty hand wipes his mouth and he reaches for his check.

The church doors open. The Bus Driver digs into his pocket.

Here you go, take these quarters, he says to Morgan. Get yourself a soda. Let us talk a bit.

Morgan skips off toward the gas station.

Mary lets out a frustrated sigh.

Things are getting worse, she says. Not that they're really getting any meaner. I don't know if that's possible. But everything happens so much faster now. And that frightens me.

Yes, he says. Remember, every bad means some good. Somewhere, at least. Somehow.

Why test them this way, she asks.

Because they have to earn it, the Bus Driver says.

But to stop it all again and start over, she says. After so much they've accomplished. The lives they've built. That's worth something. They've earned that.

Yes, the Bus Driver says. That's true. That's all true. But shouldn't they get a shot at it all on their own? From a clean start.

I just want them to stop hurting each other, she says.

If they didn't hurt each other, they couldn't love each other, he says. That's how it works.

So you'll give up on them, she asks.

That's entirely up to them, he says.

Grabbing two bags of trash, The Boy walks out the back door of the diner. When the door slams shut behind him, it startles the Devil, slipping a worn leather bag beneath the dumpster. The Boy doesn't see him there.

Each taking a moment to glance up at the stars, they both take a happy and satisfied breath.

Giving the Passengers their checks leaves The Girl one customer. She bats her eyes at Irene.

Do me another favor, The Girl asks.

Irene realizes she's stuck with a skinny, drunk man in a safety-orange hunting cap at the counter.

Fine, sure, whatever, Irene says. But now you really owe me.

Yeah, yeah, The Girl says.

Finding her book bag, she takes two quick hops around the counter and heads for the parking lot.

Throwing open the door to The Boy's car, she swings the bag into the back seat, crashes down and kisses him.

You're excited, he says.

I'm happy, she says.

FIVE - PLATE GLASS DIORAMA

Inside the diner, the Reverend stifles a giggle, finishing her cup of coffee. Her pale companion has his hands folded, looking impatient. He knows precisely how to make her laugh.

They watch a Trucker in a corner booth, all the way at the other end of the diner, who watches Irene as she buzzes past their table.

He fidgets with his silverware as Irene meanders over a stack of pancakes and some toast, accepting with a grin.

He's really got a thing for that one, the pale man says. To each his own, I guess.

Stop it, the Reverend whispers into her cup. You and your imagination.

A dollar says he's thinking maybe the next time she comes around he's going to give her a look that moves right through her, the pale man says. Maybe he'll put his hand on hers when she reaches for his plate, and he'll dazzle her with something like, you're lovely. Or maybe, lonely? Maybe she will feel his hand on her shoulder as she makes her way past his table and turn to find herself in his arms. Or maybe he'll just wait until she gets off work, finish his coffee and go home like he probably always does. Touching, really.

Hush, the Reverend whispers. Be nice.

Irene stops to pour the Reverend more coffee, eyeing her funny. As she leans across him to reach her cup, the pale man winks.

She couldn't resist me, he says. If she could see me.

The Reverend bites her lip.

Thank you very much, she says as Irene drops the check and turns toward the man across the diner.

I'll bet the first time he came in it was just for coffee and maybe some pie, the pale man says.

Irene fills the guy in the corner booth's cup and clomps away.

But it's that waitress that keeps him coming back, he says. See how she wears one of those pink waitress-type uniforms with the frill at the bottom? That's his thing, I'm telling you. Irene is the name on her blouse. Irene the mean? Irene the dream? He wants to know. Irene the queen, he imagines, because she looks like a princess to him.

The Reverend chuckles.

Trust me, I'm very, very good at this, he says.

Mitchell's right. Every time the nervous Trucker pulled into town, he spent a few hours in a corner booth at the diner, just picking up clues about the waitress named Irene. Sometimes, he drove hundreds of miles out of his way, picking up his route the next morning without telling anyone. She got off every night at a quarter until two, so it always worked out, and he never lost time. Earlier that night, he decided to finally make his move.

Irene works her way past the metal-trimmed tables, wiping and cleaning.

Tonight, maybe he'd drop a quarter into the jukebox selector at his booth. Maybe not. What sort of thing would she like? He didn't know. The Trucker looks at his watch. The place just wasn't right. Too bright. Too shiny. Behind the counter, the rims around the cushions on the stools, the edges around the walls. Bouncing florescence. Tubes of bees. Not romantic. Windows like big mirrors. Not how it was in his mind. Sitting there looking at himself doesn't do anything for his courage.

At the counter, the drunk Hunter burps over his eggs. He didn't bother to take off his big orange hunting vest. Or his sidearm. A fork hits the floor. When Irene bends for it, the old drunk is still sober enough to notice.

The Trucker in the corner booth shifts, agitated as Irene rounds the counter toward him, grinding her gum below a heavy, end-of-day glaze.

Anything else, she asks.

The nervous Trucker locks up tight and skids. Irene stares back at him.

Well, she asks.

Nah, he mumbles, slack-jawed, shifting his eyes between her and the floor. She reaches for his cup.

There's a noise behind her at the counter, like water out of a bucket. Eggs and bourbon coat both the floor and man, now moaning with his head in his hands. No one moves. A happy, neon-faced clock ticks.

The Trucker in the corner booth blinks up at Irene as she glares at the old drunk in disgust. The Trucker doesn't know what to do, so he puts his hand on her hand, still frozen to his cup on the table. Irene glances down at him in surprise. He smiles.

The Reverend drops a few dollars on the table and quickly gathers her things.

Caught off guard, staring down at the Trucker, Irene chuckles. The Trucker hesitates, unsure. First, he laughs a little too. Then a little more. The louder she laughs, the more he laughs. She yanks away her hand and sighs for a long moment.

An explosion beside the counter. Another.

The drunk is on his feet, staggering toward them. Mostly toothless. Angry. Hunting pistol in his hand.

Quit your laughing at me, he yells, the shots still ringing in his ears.

The first bullet from the Hunter's pistol passed directly through the Trucker's chest. The other through the window over his head. The gum drops from Irene's mouth as she throws herself back against the counter.

The pale man is stunned, hovering mid-thought at the diner door. The Reverend's eyes are shut tight, her hands over her face, reflex praying.

Well, I didn't see that coming, the pale man says.

The Trucker in the corner booth reaches out for Irene to hold him until help arrives. Irene screams, bounding over the counter and through the kitchen door with the grace of a deer. A door slams in the distance. Outside the window, she crosses the parking lot's circular glow, never looking back.

The Trucker in the corner booth watches her go, confused, then falls dead across the table. The drunk Hunter sits himself up on a stool, puts his gun on the counter and belches.

We should go, the Reverend says and pushes through the door.

The pale man in the suit takes a few steps toward the corner booth.

You might as well come with us, he says.

The Trucker doesn't move.

Really, it's no fun watching them cart you off, the pale man says.

The Trucker lifts his head, fuddled.

Come on, the pale man says.

The Trucker stumbles to his feet.

Wait, wait, don't look down, the pale man says, taking the Trucker by the shoulders and stepping with him toward the door.

Actually, know what, he says. Go ahead and look.

The Trucker gasps at his own dead body.

You would have hated me if I hadn't let you see that, the pale man says, leading the Trucker out the door and towards the idling bus.

The Bus Driver heard the gun shots while stepping off

the bus to double check the gas cap. The bus was already running, and the sound was similar to when it backfires. Nobody noticed at all. As he rounds the bus, his eyes linger on the glass-front diorama of a midnight murder at the Paradise Diner. He mutters absently to himself.

Damn it, he says.

SIX - DINNER KILLED THE BUDDHA

Earlier that day, before finding George waiting for him in the breakroom, the Bus Driver arrives in town too early for work. He crosses the street toward the bus station door. Brick fronts blend into an open stretch aimed at the next town. Farmers drag feed to a dirty pickup. Late summer sun sets. Lights rise from storefronts.

The Bus Driver steps up onto the curb. His reflection in the glass matches his face to the rest of his day. He yanks the door. Warm breath and fluorescence wash over him. The waiting room buzzes with boredom. Hard plastic chairs. Clock hands thumping eyelids blocking newsprint and a spotted tile floor.

The door falls shut. He's still outside.

Across the street, a beer sign flashes. The Bus Driver crosses and pulls open the door. Rows of mostly empty booths. Ceiling fans in low orbit. Dim. Cool.

He sits at the bar next to a man wearing the collar of a priest, fixated by a shrinking ice cube in a tall glass of bourbon.

Evening, the Bus Driver says and orders a cup of coffee.

The Priest doesn't hear him. After a while, the ice gives way to liquid. He leans away from the bar and sighs.

That's that, he says.

The Priest lifts a small gym bag leaning against his stool, downs the liquor, and heads for the bathroom.

The Bus Driver sips his coffee. The former priest emerges in street clothes and orders another bourbon. Gone is the collar and dark suit.

Evening, he says to the Bus Driver, resting a legal pad covered in ink on the bar.

They sit there for a while.

New shirt, the Bus Driver asks.

My Wife bought me this shirt, the man says. A long time ago.

I'm sorry, the Bus Driver says. I assumed . . .

Assume away, he says, waving the cross with both hands, then finds his glass.

The Bartender bounces off a chair behind the bar.

Yes, Father, he asks.

No, no, the man says. Don't get up. Just blessing the hell out of your bar.

Why, thank you, Father, the Bartender says.

Let me ask you something, the Bus Driver says, nodding toward the bag at the man's feet.

Alright, the man says.

Where does it all go wrong, the Bus Driver asks.

No idea, the man says. I once passed out in a corn field with a shotgun and the satisfied notion that I'd shot the moon. Doesn't leave you feeling in a good position to judge.

Nice to meet you, the Bus Driver says.

You too, says Jack Eddy.

They shake hands.

Later, bouncing through the night behind the wheel, the Bus Driver glances into his mirror to see Jack Eddy intently scribble onto his yellow legal pad through thin light above him.

Heavy raindrops. The Bus Driver finds the wipers. Deep clouds swallow the moon. Nothing beyond the headlights.

Jack Eddy slides his pen into his pocket and rubs his eyes. The pad of paper falls shut. Reaching into another pocket, he finds a frigid circle of metal. He leaves it there.

As the bus thunders on, the low vibration works its way back into the travelers' knees and knuckles. Eddy flips open his notebook and reads an inky smear of careful words:

Each member of every generation is dealt to the same way.

Options arrive face down the whole way around the table.

We weigh odds like reaching blind into a drawer full of knives. Wagers based on hunches built from confident notions. Sometimes to find fortune. Sometimes not.

Each set of players brings self-confidence born of convenience. Making jealous choices. Learning just a little bit more and passing little of it on.

Right before they call, their chair worn out, lights burrowing holes into their minds, every player has the same moment.

Their eyes fix on the markings and shapes they schemed and traded for. Relied on. Sacrificed over. And it occurs to them right then that they do not know which game they're playing at all.

Jack Eddy closes the notebook and shuts his eyes.

You know, you're actually lucky, the pale man in the black suit tells the dead Trucker, staring vacantly out the bus window. There are worse ways. Or weirder, at least.

Sitting across the aisle from them, the Reverend ignores him and pages through her bible.

You know what killed Houdini, pale man asks. Somebody punched him in the stomach too hard.

The Trucker moans and leans his head against the seat in front of him.

What's your name, bud, pale man asks.

Ernie, Ernie says.

Nice to meet you, pale man says. My name's Mitchell. Ernie, do you know what killed the Buddha?

No, Ernie says.

Bad pork, Mitchell says. Dinner killed the Buddha.

Ernie absently scratches behind his ears.

Andy Warhol was routine gall bladder surgery, Mitchell says.

I've got a question, Ernie says.

What's that, E, Mitchell asks.

Are we going to heaven, Ernie asks.

Mitchell fiddles with the knot on his deeply dyed tie,

smugly confused.

Um, he says. Well, were we good this year? No, wait, that's Christmas.

Ernie's bottom lip quivers.

No, hey, wait, no, I'm just kidding, Mitchell says. I have no idea. Really. None. Honest. It's like . . . I don't know, like your car breaks down so you get out and start walking.

Are you an angel, Ernie asks.

No, Mitchell says. But I sure sing that way.

When you die, angels come and fly you to heaven, Ernie says.

Don't believe everything you read, Mitchell says.

Then what the hell is going on here, Ernie asks.

Mitchell shrugs. They stare at each other for a long moment.

Rain again pounds the bus. None of the mostly sleeping Passengers raise their heads to look at the windows. The Reverend slides to the aisle and turns on the light over her head.

What about you, Ernie asks. Are you not an angel too?

She smiles at the dead Trucker.

No, she's the picture of health, Mitchell says.

Ernie sticks his head out into the aisle.

Driver, he yells. Anybody?

The Bus Driver bites his lip and says nothing.

They can't hear you, and don't make a ruckus, Mitchell says. If you manage to figure out how to knock the hat off of one of these people, somebody's going to get up, start screaming, running around. Pretty soon the bus'll turn over, and we'll be up to our chins in freaked-out deceased.

The Reverend slams shut her bible. Ernie crosses his arms and bangs his head against the seat in front of him.

Crap, Ernie says.

Easy, Mitchell says. Not in front of the Reverend.

Can she hear me, Ernie asks.

Yes, Mitchell says.

Then why won't she talk to me, Ernie asks.

She can't, Mitchell says.

Why, Ernie asks.

Because everybody else will think she's nuts, Mitchell says.

If she sees ghosts, she is nuts, Ernie says and looks sick, turning down the aisle. I have to go to the bathroom.

Ernie stumbles to the back of the bus. Mitchell follows him, landing on an armrest near the bathroom door when Ernie ducks inside. The bus rocks. The door shuts.

Last week a guy in Ohio was nearly killed by spare change in his shower, Mitchell says loudly. The bus rocks. The door swings open.

Who what, Ernie asks, reemerging from the bathroom, confused.

Didn't have to go, Mitchell asks.

No, not really, Ernie says.

You'll find your instincts change quite a bit, Mitchell says.

Ernie leans back against the wall.

What's in Ohio, he asks.

This guy, Mitchell says. Every time he takes a shower, pennies pour down at him from out of nowhere. Right out of nowhere. Fills the tub. Nobody knows from where. Nobody knows why. But some of them zing in pretty fast. Make it work with other people around and he'd make a million bucks. But they only show up when he's the only one there. It's getting bad. His last shower put him in the hospital. Pretty ugly.

The two stagger back down the aisle.

So, Ernie asks.

So, that's where we're going, Mitchell says. You're coming with us, aren't you?

Why, Ernie asks.

Because she's the Reverend, Mitchell says. She sees us. It runs in her family. Her Grandmother would only talk to people like us. We're the only kind of people she ever liked.

What kind of people is that, Ernie asks.

Dead people, Mitchell says.

Oh, Ernie says.

Somebody is dropping those pennies on that guy, Mitchell says. Somebody like us. And she'll talk them out of it. That's her thing. And she's great at it.

Why, Ernie asks.

Twenty-five hundred dollars, Mitchell says.

The Reverend coughs. Clears her throat. Knits her brow.

She thinks she's too classy to talk money, Mitchell says. I'm trying to get her to bump it up a bit. Really. It's a legitimate service. Ghost-be-gone.

Gone where, Ernie asks.

Mitchell twists around to look at the Reverend. She shrugs.

If she knows, she's not telling, Mitchell says. She's stubborn like that. Heaven, maybe. Hell, probably. The bottom of the ocean. The moon. I don't know, they just take off, and that's that.

What about you then, Ernie asks. Why don't you take off?

She says I must not be ready, Mitchell says.

Can she see the future, Ernie asks.

I used to think so, Mitchell says. But I doubt it. We play a lot of cards. If she knew the future, she'd bluff a little better.

Maybe she's bluffing that she's bad at bluffing, Ernie says.

Mitchell hadn't thought of this.

The Reverend smiles. She likes Ernie.

SEVEN - JIMMY'S BURGERS

As the bus burrows further into the night, Irv and Johnny spot the words *Alexa Jenkins Wins Again* spray-painted across a road sign.

Johnny laughs. The bus rumbles along.

Irv looks over.

What are you smiling at, he asks.

Oh, nothing, Johnny says. Back home, this girl. Her name is spray-painted on the dark side of this bunch of rocks in the middle of this half of a river near where we live. Funny, the things you think about all of a sudden sometimes. The sunlight hits that spot only late in the afternoon during the summer, which makes it a really cold place to swim out to. But a great place to smoke marijuana. Linda liked that rock and called it the testament to her immortality. When my buddy Jake, who we call Mud, waded out to paint it, he was in water that still had big chunks of ice floating around. She was the only girl our age from someplace else. Some big city. Can't remember which one. She had spiky hair. About a million earrings. She knew about bands. Mud and I had a running bet about whether she had a tattoo. And also one about where. We'd invite her down to the river whenever we could. But she'd say the water was too cold to swim. So we'd end up just staring at her lying on the bank, sunning herself. It's a nice spot. Gave you a chance to think about stuff. This one time, our friend William started asking what we think Hell is.

In the middle of a long afternoon, Mud and Johnny have their backs to William and the sun, feet in the water. Both turn around to squint at him.

Not like theologically, William says. Seriously. What actually would it be?

I don't know, Johnny says.

Mud sets his eyes back on Linda.

What if it's just like this, William says. What if it's a big river. But the river's really cold all the time, like almost freezing, but never turning to ice. And every couple of feet are rocks with people on them. All the rocks are just barely too far apart to jump to without touching water. It's really cloudy, so when you get wet, you really never get dry. You're already dead, so even though there isn't any food, you can't starve. You are out there forever, and there isn't anything to do but jump from rock to rock and freeze your ass off.

Yeah, Johnny says. But you don't have any shoes, and the rocks are really rough.

Yeah, William says. But, look, there would be rough rocks and really rough rocks. And no matter where you are, there's always the chance of getting just a little more comfortable. So all these people would come along and try to push you off your rock because they think it's better than theirs.

You would do the same thing, Mud says.

I sure would, William says.

That would suck, Johnny says.

Yeah, says William.

Mud and Linda wave at each other. The sun in her eyes, she puts up a hand for shade. Mud makes a motion with one hand and points toward some trees with the other.

What are you telling her, Johnny asks.

Nothing, Mud says. I'm just screwing around. But watch.

Linda waves her hands and does the same sort of thing, pointing at the water. If he's going to bluff, so is she.

Mud, for some reason, picked this girl out as an ideal,

Johnny tells Irv, as the bus hums along. Linda wasn't so much who he wanted, but more what he wanted. Kind of a general blueprint. Don't ask me why. She was a pretty silly girl as girls go.

She thinks I'm saying stuff, Mud says. It's really funny.
Bet she's thinking the same thing about you, Johnny says.
That would be cool, Mud laughs.

Mud, William, Linda, and I lived in what we call The Suburb For No Apparent Reason, Johnny tells Irv. Our entire hometown is, for all intents and purposes, two rows of buildings on either side of a long road connecting the Pennsylvania Turnpike to nowhere in particular. All the place does is serve the area with a post office and a county seat, a high school and a grocery store. There's also a big plant a couple miles away that makes paper, so everything around it stinks like something that couldn't decide whether to die or not. Some fool built four rows of townhouses up on a hill at the end of a long gravel road, as if somebody accidentally dropped them there while carrying them somewhere else and never bothered to go back and get them. Some kind of investment scheme. The guy went to jail. They aren't even in straight lines, but shoot out in weird, crooked directions along the hill. Nobody ever got around to planting grass or trees. But, anyway, I guess everybody's from someplace.

I got all my college stuff back in the mail, William says as the sun sets across the rocks.
We all got that stuff a while ago, Mud says.
No, scholarship stuff, William says. I didn't get any.
Any, Johnny asks.
Not enough, William says.

You'll figure something out, Mud says, climbing down off the rock. They wade out toward the bank where Linda's waiting. William calls Johnny and Mud over to where he's looking into the water.

Look, William says, pointing. Those two sticks look like a guy walking down the side of a big tree.

Johnny and Mud wade over to William. The current breaks around those rocks in the black-green-brown water. A huge tree limb jammed itself there. Right near the surface they could see a really cool twist where two separate branches grew together a long time ago. Where the knot pokes toward the sky, what looks like a barrel-chested something with a flat head carries a basket full of fellow driftwood down into wherever he was going, balancing on a couple of long, thin legs.

What's he carrying, Mud asks.

What do you mean, William asks.

He's holding something over his head, Johnny says.

That is his head, William says.

No, look, his head is flat and tucked under, and his arms wrap up around, Johnny says.

Yeah, I can see that, says William. But I figured his arms are crossing his chest.

Mud puts his face an inch from the water.

He's walking out, he says. You know, out of the water.

They all lean in and squint, stoned, noses dipping in the current. There is a long moment with no noise. No wind.

My Parents have no idea I do drugs, Mud says.

Cutting up through the woods toward home, they cross a dirt and gravel field along railroad tracks, below the lurching neighborhood. Linda splits off toward her house with a wave.

Later losers, she says.

Johnny walks ahead, head tipped back, watching stars pop one by one by one. Mud and William trudge a couple steps behind, Mud lecturing that after a while a person makes their way off the river in Hell and the next part was finding their shoes and walking home with dirt and rocks in their socks.

Can you earn your way out of Hell, you think, William asks.

How the hell should I know, asks Mud.

They laugh at that.

Later that night, Johnny leaned in the doorway of what used to be a major chain restaurant parked off the nearest freeway cloverleaf, watching his two best friends toss trash bags full of meat into a big blue dumpster. The oddly shaped building became, at some point, the Big Jim Davis Burger House. Colors switched. Signs painted over or altered just enough to pass. Which sells just enough burgers to stay open, but too few to keep from throwing half the meat away every week.

Mud and William have six or so trash bags full of meat and other stuff, hiking hammer-throw style across the parking lot and into the dumpster. William reverses. Mud fakes. William slams it home. A couple long throws. They chase the bags, lumbering down into a drainage ditch. Johnny leans there and watches them under the security light in the corner of the parking lot, laughing. Not thinking, not doing anything at all.

Jimmy's Burgers sits in a better place to put a speed trap than a restaurant. Plus, it still looked pretty much like what it was built as in the first place. They spent half their time trying to explain why they couldn't make a Whopper.

Right then Johnny didn't have to move. Didn't have to talk. When they got done, they'd all go back inside and do something else. No need to plan for it. The air was warm and they didn't have to go back to high school. Still a lot left to the summer.

When Mud's Father died, they were all fourteen. Mud's

Uncle showed up with shovels and they buried him themselves. The way Johnny felt in that moment, when they all looked at each other and walked out of the graveyard, was exactly the same way he felt that night out by the dumpster at Jimmy's.

Johnny wanders back inside. Linda is yelling for him. She's working the front counter all by herself. They're out of fries. He grabs the rusty wire basket.

A Traveling Family waits. Tired. A long way from anywhere. Pants, shirts glued to their skin. The Mom simmers. She yelled at the unlit and clearly-marked-as-broken order sign in the drive-thru lane for ten minutes. A complete and intricate order she repeated multiple times.

The youngest caterwauls, going all squirmy when his Father tries to pick him up. The other one, a little girl, is face down, asleep on the floor, barefoot. Johnny puts the bags together. Mom checks each one carefully.

Meanwhile, James Davis himself grumbles in a little office behind a door next to the grill, morning, noon and night, watching evangelists on a tiny, fuzzy television.

The Husband-Dad guy, Johnny tells Irv. He was standing there half-asleep and drooping. A kid squirming over one shoulder, another one asleep on his shoe. With these terrible khaki pants and running shoes. Little arms. Big belly. Is it weird that I feel like I can do that? Like, I'd be good at that?

The Mom scoops one kid off the tile. The Dad hauls the other out the door like a sack of potatoes. Linda climbs onto a stool in the little glass drive-thru window closet that they never use.

Why Mud, Linda asks.

Why not Mud, Johnny asks.

No, I mean his name, Linda says, picking at a fingernail. Where does that name Mud come from?

Instead of buying ketchup packets, Jimmy went to an auction and got an always-clogged gadget with Century Condiment Company Dispensation Unit printed across a fading metallic sticker on the side. A real money saver of mismatched nozzles, plastic canisters and tubes. Johnny grabs the spout and pulls it to pieces.

It was a joke when we were kids, Johnny says. One day, somebody said, like, you know, the thing in a cartoon where somebody says, your name is Mud and Mud spelled backwards is dumb. Well, the joke is that he was so stupid his name spelled backward is Mud. Just stuck.

You guys are weird, she says.

Johnny hides the pump under some stuff in the sink so that the dayshift will have to scrape it out.

He's not stupid, Linda says, sipping on a soda she'd hidden under the counter.

No, but it was also the day they caught him eating cat food, Johnny says.

Linda stares at the counter, bobbing at the knees.

He ate a lot of it, he says. A whole cat's worth.

She's not listening to him.

You sure like him a lot, he says. Don't you?

Who, Linda asks.

Mud, Johnny says.

I don't know, she says. But he likes me.

In the kitchen, William sits on boxes full of cola syrup, eating a dripping hamburger. Mud cuts labels off of cans of ketchup and pickles with his penknife and switches them to screw up the dayshift.

To me, Heaven is a peanut butter and jelly sandwich when you're stoned, Mud says, shoving a can of relish, marked mustard, onto a higher shelf.

No, William says between bites. It's like how my Grandfather lives. He's seventy. He worked all of his life and now he's done. So he sits in his basement, watches TV, smokes cigars, and my Grandma calls him for meals. Other than that, people come by and they play cards. There is not an old person that he doesn't talk to or anybody that he doesn't know.

William stares at the floor, lost.

Don't know how you get to that, he says.

Mud shakes his head.

Look, he says. What is your damage lately?

Johnny plants himself in the corner.

I tell you, it's two things, William says, wiping his hands on his pants. It's this Danny thing, and it's this college thing. Both of them seem to be things I should be worried about, but I can't seem to concentrate on either of them. My mind wanders.

Danny was this kid a year older than us that moved away in ninth grade, Johnny tells Irv as they roll past a village of fast food and cheap gas. Last year, he jumped out of a plane and died. We heard it from one of my Mom's friends, who didn't really know exactly what had happened. His parachute didn't open or something. It was sad, but only in a faraway way.

The Danny thing bugs me because he was around our age and I figured I'd see him at some point again, William says. Somebody'd run into him or something, and there he'd be. I think of everybody that way. It's weird. And I really don't know how to pay for college, so the whole future thing is going all fuzzy on me. And like I said, my mind keeps wandering away from figuring out what to do.

Look, thinking about the future is easy, Mud says. The future is like a bourbon milkshake. Sure, it sounds nasty, but bourbon is good and milk is good and ice cream is good. So how bad could it be?

Jimmy closes early on Sundays. Sundays are particularly

slow. Instead of driving straight home, the guys take a long road that curves out through the county and ends up in town, so they could get stoned and then drive some to air out Mud's Brother's car on the way back.

So what are you going to do, Mud asks.

Mud, I don't think he wants to talk about it, says Johnny from the back seat.

You must have some sort of backup plan or something, Mud says.

Like what, William asks.

I don't know, something, Mud says. Got to be something.

The car curves into darkness.

I don't think he wants to talk about it, Johnny says.

I could join the Navy, William says.

You can't be in the Navy, Mud says.

Anybody can be in the Navy, William says. It's the Navy.

You quit the Boy Scouts because they were too bossy, Mud says. And guys with crew cuts always want to punch you. It's chemical.

I've got to do something, William says. He digs under the passenger seat and pops in one of Mud's Brother's tapes. A low hiss. Johnny stretches his legs across the back seat, his head on the armrest, and watches the moon follow the car. The tape kicks over to the other side.

You could drive a truck, Johnny says. You could make a good living that way, doing something like that. That's what they say on those commercials. Call now!

They didn't hear him over the wind and sudden Sabbath screeching out over the back-left speaker.

I might stay here, William says, popping out the tape. There are jobs at the plant.

No, Mud says. No way you can roll paper all your life. We all have to get out of here. All of us.

Johnny closes his eyes and tries to tell if they were driving past tree rows or open fields by the wind whipping past the windows. He likes it there.

I like it here, William says.

Yeah, well, neat, you can visit on holidays, Mud says. Poor dumb people with no idea what they're doing and nowhere to go is the foundation on which this town is founded. This is zero. This is where you start, and then you go somewhere else.

So what do I do, William asks.

Figure it out, Mud says. I don't know. Let's start over. What do you want to be when you grow up?

I don't know, William says. Happy?

Aim higher, Mud says.

Rich, William asks.

That's the stuff, Mud says.

He puts the car in park at the stoplight on Main Street to concentrate on yelling at William.

I don't think he wants to talk about it anymore, Johnny says.

William is starting to sulk. Johnny sits up to stretch.

The town's first stoplight, historically speaking, is down the hill from there, in front of the courthouse, Johnny tells Irv. For years it was the only one, until our houses were built. Then they put in this other one. Everybody ignores it, but we'd never run it with dope in the car.

Down the hill, a mechanical roar. A primer-colored muscle car grumbles impatiently at the other stoplight, offering a column of thick, gray smoke. Next to the car at the light hums a little yellow station wagon.

The light changes. The muscle car's tires scream and spin. Engine moaning, the sound avalanches toward them. With a lurch, the big gray car tears up the street, bounding over bad spots in the blacktop. Headlights smiling to the heavens.

The muscle car's driver white knuckles the wheel, glaring down the double yellow line. So he probably never noticed the lady in the station wagon accelerating naturally, evenly behind him, just a couple feet behind, as if following a trash truck up the street.

Jesus, Mud says.

That was the saddest thing I ever saw, William says.

It was only a few moments later, as they climbed out of Mud's Brother's car outside his house, that three friends distracted by the future came to the same realization at the same time: We forgot to smoke marijuana.

EIGHT - CENTER OF THE UNIVERSE

Many miles after the bus leaves the Paradise Diner, Jack Eddy still feels his breakfast settling. The fat Salesman elbows him for the millionth time.

Hey, ever hear the one about when all the body organs argued about which one's most important, he asks.

What is it you sell again, Jack Eddy asks.

Moisture meters, the Salesman says.

What's a moisture meter for, Jack Eddy asks.

Measuring moisture, the Salesman says, yanking a card out of his pocket. Agricultural applications, mostly. Globally known.

Edgar Pence, Inside Sales, Jack Eddy reads in the dim overhead light. After staring out the window for a long while, he reaches for his notepad and pen:

Every morning since he was seven years old, The Dalai Lama says, wherever I go, with whomever I go, may I see myself as less than all others, and, from the depth of my heart, may I consider them supremely precious.

The Dalai Lama never met Edgar Pence.

In the good old days, every morning, Pence opened his eyes and smiled.

For weeks, months, he was on the road. Woke up in a Holiday Inn, went downstairs, took his coffee at the front desk. Slid into a new rental car. Across town to some dull office. Glad hands all around. A couple bathroom jokes. Then, lunch. A good one at the nice place in town.

It was simple. New product, cutting edge! Maintains moisture levels for a whole variety of crops.

You grow it, we measure it, Pence would grin.

The brilliant part? It was actually something new. Something these wholesalers and regional middle men and actual dirt farmers really needed. The darling of commodities markets everywhere.

Pence would lean knowingly across empty glasses covering a wobbly table in some plush restaurant.

Do you feel your moisture levels are proper, he'd ask, accusingly. Are they safe?

Safe, the Customers asked.

From the typical, and, if you check the numbers, appalling, damage and loss over time, Pence rambled. From the otherwise inevitable creeping rot. It's a game of inches, gentlemen. We all know that. Those inches make the mile.

Sweating into their power ties, they all reached for their checkbooks.

Hold on, Pence would caution. Just one problem. May not be enough of this cutting-edge product to go around. The waiting list is long. First come, first serve.

Couldn't Pence possibly help them out, they'd insist. Get them to the head of the line?

A few bills under the table, then off to the bar for drinks, waitresses, and occasional good fortune.

It was at a motel bar somewhere in Iowa when Pence's proper place in creation first dawned on him. It was closing time. He'd worked his way across the top shelf. Happy hour seemed like a lifetime ago, when he handed the Bartender the company credit card. As the lights came up, he found to the left of him a newly single Marketing Manager with a hotel room provided by her company. On his other side, her lovely-enough-at-this-hour Roommate, who said she liked the way he smelled. Pence ordered them another round, but the Bartender pointed to the clock.

Pence shot his cool salesman's glance across the bar. The one that said, there's a little something extra in it for you.

Wordless. Soundless. Mostly with the eyebrows. A gift, really.

One more round, the Bartender said.

The dim light twirled around him. Like Superman and the earth's yellow sun.

Know what, Pence asked.

The loose ladies leaned in close.

What, they asked.

You're looking at the center of the universe, Pence said.

You're funny, chimes his lady to the left, leaning against him in a vodka and cranberry haze.

Pence then rose to his toes in order to fully address the empty room. Drink in hand, he thrust a fist into the air. Then collapsed into a heap on the floor. The Bartender and the ladies split his cash.

Decades on the road. He bemoaned it always. So they let him take it easy whenever he got to be back at the main office. Nice and easy. Smooth and simple. It was his time to rest. The plaques and awards stretched out his office door, down the hall and through the lobby.

But then the guy with his name on the letterhead died in his car at a stoplight, with the news channel report of his very own traffic jam squawking over the radio. And along with him went much of the carte blanche Pence so very much enjoyed as official keeper of secrets from younger days.

The Old Boss told Pence about their super-confidential design flaw one night before his fourth divorce. They drank a bottle of his very expensive scotch while Pence helped him bury suitcases full of cash deep in the woods. There's this little metal pin between the backing plate and the main gears. Normally nothing to think about. Just sits there. But if that pin falls out somehow, it's only a matter of time. It's supposed to shove a lever resting in an aluminum bracket. The lever triggers a gear that resets the meter once a month.

It's only supposed to move back and forth against a rubber stopper. So it isn't fastened on the short end. If you crank the gears too hard the wrong way, it pops right out on its own. But the biggest thing they forgot to think about? Gravity. That was moisture meter 1.0's problem. It worked perfectly under all conditions. Except upside down. Which almost never happens, until it does. No way to tell anything's wrong. Wait a couple weeks. And then boom! Fancy metal doorstop.

The Old Boss blamed it on his partner. That crook. The numbers people figured that one in forty thousand would burn up on their own. It's not like they explode. They just stop working and smell like burning oil. So the people ship it back, and the company declares user error. Simple. They caught it in the fifth year. But not before moving a ton of them. So they never did publicly correct the issue. What's the use of that? Just imagine if word got out. The stock would drop, the credit would dry up, and they wouldn't even have a company.

Secrets have value, Pence's Father always said. Never forget that. Secrets have value.

And then the Old Boss's kid moved in. He used to caddy at the country club and got half a master's degree at some fancy school. Big ideas guy. No tie. Now he's the one with the center parking spot.

Which moves Pence up the ladder. The last great war horse comes home to advise and instruct future salesmen from behind a bigger desk in the dingy gray office building. The promotion placed him directly under the New Boss's thumb. Right down the hall. Set salary. Regular hours. No kickbacks. And only one decent coffee maker. Located in his kitchen at home. Next to his Wife, screaming at the kids across the breakfast table every morning. Day in, day out.

Yet now, with something to finally complain about, Pence held his tongue. Through unavoidable recitals and graduations. Backyard barbecues. Runny noses. Report cards. Busted pipes. Deep inside Pence, pressure grew. After a while, even porn didn't help.

There's a secondary flaw in such a long-lasting product which everyone needs. Eventually, everyone who needs one, has one. They shifted the ink around as long as they could, but after a while, company value tumbled. Deep cuts down the line. The Christmas party moved to the budget motel off the highway. Then to the VFW hall. Then the back room at some theme restaurant at the mall. Company cars, gone. Secretaries, gone, even the pretty ones. Expense accounts? They didn't even have a form for that anymore.

Seemed it couldn't get worse. But then the New Boss announced one morning that the whole problem was that they had nobody out there with enough experience to really sell the new designer colors and weak-kneed upgrades. The moisture alarm could now do any of six primitive cell phone rings. Who did they have left that could hit the street?

Pence was on the job. Bus tickets instead of a car to the airport. But it felt like a prison break.

What he found on the road wasn't pretty. Pence's backslapping contacts all now replaced with junior drones.

His instructions from their new, very expensive, Marketing Consultant was part pep talk, part business seminar. Pence put his age somewhere around thirteen. Show up in person, glad hands all around. Act decent. Watch the language. Reinforce company values. Plus the occasional physical exam of the product in action. They handed him a checklist on his way out the door, all outlined in a glossy, threefold pamphlet with happy cartoon clients. Similar to the ones air stewards point to while describing how to escape a burning jet plane.

We need to keep up appearances, we need to do this personally, the Consultant said to him again and again, flashing those damn bus tickets and a condescending grin.

Knock them dead, big guy, he said.

The itinerary they emailed him took him to his hometown on the day of his thirtieth high school reunion. Damn itinerary. Every morning he had to check in and report the precise time he reached each destination, along with the full name of whomever he met with and their contact information. He had to fill out a survey and so did the customer. At the bottom, they left a large space to explain why there wasn't a new order. Even the paperwork could tell this was pointless.

He got off the bus that day in the center of town and ran directly into somebody he knew in school. And another one, and another.

At the student-union cocktail hour, everyone wore their senior year portrait on a tiny name tag. Pence approached with a confident attack.

So what are you doing now, somebody asks.

A question with no good answer. Only nodding exaggerations.

Top Regional District Sales Leader Champion, practiced Pence at the bathroom mirror, straightening his tie, sucking in his gut.

He grimaces at his badge, senior yearbook photo blurred across the front. In high school, everyone called him Pie Face.

Um, great, his classmates all mumbled, then skirted off to talk to somebody else across the gymnasium.

So at the open bar, when the lights came up and the School Janitor was pushing everyone to leave, Pence grabbed the only other guy taking advantage of the Bartender.

Ever hear the one about when all the body organs argued about which one's most important, Pence slurred.

No, said the guy, Pence's Locker Buddy sophomore year.

So, Pence says. The brain goes, I think and I run everything. And the stomach goes, I'm the one that digests food. And the lungs go . . . You get it?

Yeah, his Locker Buddy said, not interested.

And after a couple days, the organs feel all woozy, Pence said. Sick. Know why? They realize the body hasn't crapped in a week. Why? Get this. Because every body needs an asshole.

Nice, the guy said, wandered in a circle for a moment, looked a little sick, then stumbled away. Pence laughed completely of his own accord and shuffled his ice cubes at the Bartender.

It's the asshole, Jack Eddy says, as the bus burrows on into the night. Everybody needs an asshole.

Man, you can really ruin a joke, pal, Pence says.

Now a little grumpy, Pence closes his eyes and thinks back to the thick metal housing of every single one of the company moisture meters that he laid his hands on over the course of this long, tedious trip.

The conversations with every faceless Customer fell into a regular pattern.

Hey, while you're filling out that survey, mind if I go back and write down the numbers on the side of your moisture unit, Pence asked. For our records. I need to put it on the form. Just takes a second. Thanks.

Everybody needs an asshole, Pence chuckles to no one in particular, drifting off to sleep with the entire trip's worth of OKH200 center pins yanked from soon-to-fail moisture meters, clipped on a key ring, tucked in his top pocket.

NINE - THE CHURCH OF LARRY

The bus slows at a tiny, dark transfer stop along the side of the road. The skies are open again and pouring down in sheets.

As the doors split, a teenager with a pair of metal suitcases crashes into one of the front seats, drenched to the bone. He sticks where he lands like a wad of gum. Without moving another muscle, he's fast asleep.

Falling asleep in the front seat of a giant, cream-colored Lincoln two days before. Bare feet on the dash. Windows rolled down. A dry, warm wind pouring across Mexico and up his pant leg. Traveling seemed like the best thing in the world. He just closed his eyes and drifted away.

And until a bump in the highway five miles from Texas jostled him awake, it didn't occur to him that his friend may or may not be crying.

Larry, I can't go to Houston, man, his College Roommate said, squeezing the wheel hard with both hands.

There was a plane home from Houston. The plan was, drop the Lincoln at the guy's relatives' house and get to the airport with time to spare. So, a little surprised, Larry sat up.

Why not, Larry asks.

It took less than a mile to unfold a bundle of heartache with both of them caught at the center.

Instead of Houston, the car was going north to a town outside Reno, to the house of the guy's high school girlfriend, who may or may not still be in love with him.

The only question now was whether one or both of them were going there along with it. She was leaving to study abroad. There was no time to lose.

Flying to Mexico to bring a classic luxury car back over the border, with a semester of college trailing behind him, and his Roommate showing him the Texas countryside, seemed like a good idea two weeks before. Sure beat a part-time job and paper hat.

So he took an advance on his birthday money and flew away. And even at that moment, rolling through Mexico, digesting this new information, it was still quite a while before any sort of panic set in.

But when the Lincoln left Larry in a pool of light outside a train station many miles southwest of Houston later that night, reality bared its teeth.

Compromise brought them at least this far. To a remote parking lot where major interstates split. They saw a sign along the road for this train depot. That settled it.

I'm so sorry about this, man, Larry's Roommate said, hurrying back into the car. But I gotta go. See you at school.

A-hole, Larry grumbled through a smile, waving his friend a safe voyage.

Larry'd already blown through all of his cash. As a show of peace, his Roommate forked over whatever was in his pockets, which wasn't much.

In theory, all was fine. The plane didn't leave until the next day. In theory, the airport was just a couple hours away. In theory, it was all so clearly worked out as they shook hands and swore that there were no hard feelings. That they would see each other soon.

Larry watched his friend disappear. It was quiet out there. He found his phone somewhere at the bottom of his luggage and tapped. The phone blinked once and died. Larry blinked twice and tapped harder. It wasn't until this moment he remembered the phone's long fall to the motel bathroom floor and tricky, slow-motion bounce behind the toilet. Though his primary concern was goo and germs, it turns out that wasn't his main problem. He held it up to the light and could see the screen was cracked. He tapped. Nothing. Again. Nothing. Again . . . Nothing. Larry took a frustrated breath and turned to find the little train depot closed.

At this moment, Larry's mind traveled outside him. It rose high in the air, chasing the car that left him. Diving through the roof, his mind lands in the glovebox, where they'd been keeping his only credit card. The one they were using for gas. The big car meant they stopped a lot, and Larry got tired of digging it out of his wallet every time. Larry's mind returned to him with the sound and feeling of glass breaking.

No trains this time of night, said the nearest Gas Station Attendant, a half mile away. You don't got Uber?

My phone isn't really working, Larry said. Is there maybe a fixit place, or . . .

The Attendant laughed and shuffled back into his tiny office.

The fluorescent domes at the top of the gas pumps anchored a colliding galaxy of insects. A fly strip peppered with petrified corpses dangled from the frame of the cashier's door, swaying in the slight wind. Spoiled fuel and whiffs of pine tree air freshener mixed in the crystal-clear darkness surrounding the tiny isle of light. The silence sounded just like screaming. The weight of the moment enough to crush him. But he picked up his bag and started walking. First in one direction. Then the other. Then he put his suitcases down. And picked them up again, taking two steps toward a man standing a few feet away at the gas pump.

Uhm, hello, which way to Houston, Larry sputtered.

With braided, gray hair, the man pumped fuel into the

tail of a long silver Cadillac, U.S. and Texas flags flying from the rear windows. Gazing over at Larry, he chewed on a toothpick as the numbers on the pump spun.

Need a ride, he asked.

Twelve years of cautionary health-class filmstrips sloshed back toward Larry.

Uhm, he said, losing all the feeling in his hands where they cramped around the suitcase handles. Yeah, sure, I guess, yeah.

Out on the highway, a loose wire in the dome light flickered with the tires whirring in even time against the road. The Cadillac's front seat was just as roomy as the Lincoln. Maybe more so. But with the overwhelming feeling of being in somebody else's living room, Larry was by no means comfortable.

A Mexican radio station whispered out of the dash. A statue of St. Anthony swung by his feet from the rearview mirror. The man's toothpick swung back and forth between the corners of his mouth.

After a while, Larry let his suitcases slide onto the floor from where he clutched them in his lap. In a few minutes more, maybe an hour or an hour and a half, he would be where he needed to be. Perhaps then he could find an empty bench and just wait a while. It was a thought that usually would have seemed impossible to him, spending the night on an airport bench. But it was really, right then, all that he wanted in the world.

It was at that moment that the stranger beside him told him to loosen up.

What, Larry asked.

You're wound up like a steel spring over there, he said. Making me jitter. Cool it.

The more Larry thought about it, the more it seemed like he should find the correct thing to say. After a while, the feeling passed.

I don't know if I can, Larry said.

Look, the man said. You know how there's the stuff you can control. And then there's the stuff you can't?

Yeah, Larry said.

So, then cool it, he said, rolling down the window a little to throw out his toothpick. He pulled another from his shirt pocket and opened the glove compartment, handing Larry a flyer.

It reads: *Church of Marvin*. On the other side, the single word was *Surrender*.

Church of Marvin, Larry asked.

That's right, Marvin said. And Susan. She's got one too.

Who's Susan, Larry asked.

My Wife, Marvin said.

Alright, Larry said. So . . .

You'll see, Marvin said. You'll see. Just keep watching.

I will, Larry asked.

Do you want to, Marvin asked.

Sure, Larry said.

Marvin took the toothpick out of his mouth and tapped it against the steering wheel.

What's your name, he asked.

Larry, Larry said.

Well, there you go, Marvin said. The Church of Larry. Welcome.

Thanks, Larry said.

A few hours later, the Cadillac pulled up to a motel not far from the airport. Waving through the car window after climbing out and gathering his bags, Larry watched Marvin point to his nose with a nod and vanish into the night.

In a wrinkled envelope, Larry's plane ticket had 4 p.m. printed in red across the top. A time many hours away. He did math in his head for a long while. With the small wad of bills still resting in the other pocket, Larry took a deep

breath and rang the bell on the motel office door. Lights
went on and a bedraggled Motel Manager in a terry cloth
bathrobe slid open a narrow security window.

Room, the Manager asked.

Yeah, Larry said.

Hour, the Manager asked.

I don't know, Larry said. It's late. My phone broke.

No, do you want it for the whole hour, the Manager
asked.

Until morning, actually, Larry said.

I'll have to charge you the whole rate, the Manager said.

That's fine, Larry said and counted out way more than
half of all his money in the world.

It took a while to turn the lock on his room's thick door.
A chain-smoking guy in a sleeveless t-shirt slouching in a
folding chair outside the next room cheered and coughed
when it snapped open at last.

Larry dropped his suitcases and plopped down on the
bed. The room smelled like air that never moved and a bible
propped up a leg on the night stand. A dim haze spreading
from the overhead light faded across thin orange carpet.
Larry reached the dresser and switched on a round plastic
lamp. Pitch darkness poured out of the open bathroom
door, wrestled with the lamp light and won. No TV.

Slumping back across the fuzzy bedspread, Larry stared
up at the bugs lying dead against the ceiling light's frosted
glass, their crooked legs making double shadows between
the bulbs. He watched the long hand of the bedside clock
sweep forward an hour and decided to find something to
eat. Changing into a slightly cleaner shirt, Larry pushed his
suitcases under the bed. He found his Neighbor still
smoking outside.

Is there any place to eat around here, Larry asked.

Chinese, the man said, tipping precariously backward in
his rusty chair. Other side of the overpass.

Is it still open, Larry asked.

Maybe, he said.

Thanks, Larry said.

At the end of the parking lot, Larry spotted the overpass about a quarter mile away, with bright lights glowing on the other side. All at once, he started to feel better about things. He got this far. And handled the situation fairly well.

Most of all, he was all by himself, in middle of a nice summer night, with the whole thing under control. Then, all at once, he couldn't find his room key. Not in his front pants pockets. Not in his back pockets. He couldn't even specifically remember locking the door.

Larry stopped walking, started sweating, and found the key jingling in the top pocket of his shirt, where he put it for safe keeping.

A truck stormed past out of nowhere and startled him. He watched it go and started again toward the overpass. He worried about his suitcases back in the room. He'd left the bathroom window wide open. Why even bother locking the door? Stupid. Probably too tiny to crawl through, but still.

In any case, Larry did have his ticket and wallet on him, so he told himself to relax.

Just as this was easing his mind, the street light above him went out and he fell beneath the electrical shade of the overpass. It took a moment for his eyes to adjust.

There was a shape like a grocery cart and another like a person lying in the gutter. But as he walked by them, the person became a discarded rug and the cart a drooping cardboard box. Dark streaks of shadow swept down dirty, spray-painted walls. Gang signs and cartoon portraits drifted into each other, took new shapes and disappeared. Just as Larry neared the half circle of light from the strip mall on the other side, someone in the darkness coughed.

Larry ran.

Two connected buildings sharing a sidewalk waited for

him on the other side. His choices were Chinese food delivery and same-day dry cleaning. The good one was still open. Pulling on the front door, he found it locked, though there were several people working inside.

He knocked. A tiny Elderly Woman moved toward him, waving her hands.

Go away, she said. Delivery only.

Larry didn't know what to say.

Delivery only, she said again.

A skinny Delivery Boy with a spotty teenage beard appeared at her side.

Go away, he said. Delivery only. Delivery!

Larry took the money out of his pocket and pressed it against the glass.

Police, she said to the skinny boy as he put his hand on her arm.

Delivery only, he said. Closing in five minutes! Go away!

Beaten, Larry planted his forehead against the glass.

In front of the dry cleaners, an ancient pay phone hung near the door.

The restaurant workers moved back behind the counter. Larry wondered, if he ordered food, would they drive him back to the motel? Because he'd never make it back there in time to order. Fishing spare change out of his pocket, he dialed. They answered the phone on the second ring.

Delivery, the voice said. Address?

Larry read the address off of the dry cleaner's window.

Wait, hold on, the voice on the phone said.

A thump of the phone hitting the counter. Distant multi-leveled chatter. Larry waited. Cars passed along the bridge. Five feet directly above him, a billion bugs fluttered against an industrial light bolted to the building's side. Larry wondered, when the light goes out, where must they all go? A cloud so dense, it seemed like they could swoop down and carry him away. He kind of wished they would.

A different voice picked up the phone.

Hello, the Delivery Boy said.

Yes, Larry said. I'd like to order please?

The skinny, bearded Delivery Boy pushed open the front door and stared at him through the glass.

Go away, he said into the phone, a long cord trailing behind him.

I just want to eat, Larry yelled.

No, the Delivery Boy yelled.

Larry threw his hands up, trying for desperate but not threatening.

Please, he yelled Pretty please?

The skinny boy pointed at the pay phone receiver. Larry grabbed it and ordered.

Go wait at the end of the parking lot, the Delivery Boy said and hung up.

Leaning against a telephone pole, Larry threw little rocks at a rusty paint can until his food arrived, carried in a plastic bag by his new friend.

Cash, the teenager said, holding the food away from Larry until he saw the money.

Looking past him, Larry could see a family of worried faces pressed against their front window.

Larry handed over extra. The Delivery Boy dropped the food, stuffed the money in his pocket, and sprinted back across the parking lot.

Larry had planned to sit and eat it right there, with them watching him, but then thought about the rest of the bugs he couldn't see in the dark. He looked back toward the underpass.

The sweet smell of his dinner wafted up his shirt sleeve and popped out at his neck. Halfway under the bridge, Larry panicked and broke into a run. The wind filled his ears and stung his eyes. He hadn't run since middle school. Lunging to a stop when he reached the light on the other side, out of breath, he had nothing to throw up.

Larry pushed his thick room door open, still a little out of breath. Once the lights were on, he threw the bolt and attached the door chain.

Soon stuffed with MSG, Larry rolled over onto his back, counting the rough points of the drippy stucco ceiling. But not for long.

At noon, the beige phone on the end table rang. He thought it was a fire alarm.

Check out, growled a voice as pleasant as coffee poured over gravel.

Sunlight flooded through worn drapes swishing friendly circles around the room. Larry uncurled and couldn't remember where he was.

It took him much longer than he expected to walk to the airport and cross the vast parking lot. He handed the Agent at the counter his ticket. She typed on a computer. For the first time, he felt he could breath.

This flight is tomorrow, the Ticket Agent said. You're very early.

Deep in his chest, Larry felt his heart break. His feet sunk into the floor. His hands shook. He was out of money.

Taking back his ticket, Larry stared woozily at the Agent, too tired to sigh.

A giant, steel-ribbed picture window of planes parked, taking off and landing, climbed two stories in front of him. But none of them were his.

For no reason at all, he searched his pockets. His hands had nothing better to do. The Agent behind the counter waited. The line behind him grumbled, impatient. He thought he might just drop into a puddle.

And then the crowd parted. Walking at Larry with a giant smile, the man in a bolo tie and long, gray braid down his back.

Larry, Marvin said.

Marvin, Larry said.

Marvin handed Larry a business card. Last night it looked like you might need this, he said.

On the front is printed: *Church of Larry*. On the other side: *Relax*.

Thanks, Larry said.

No problem, Marvin said as he turned back into the crowd with a wave. Have a great day.

Just then, a frustrated Personal Assistant pushed past Larry to get to the counter and said the name of Larry's hometown. There's a flight their very important and unreasonable employer desperately needed to switch to. Tomorrow. Larry tapped the simmering Assistant on the shoulder.

I happen to know about a seat that might free up, Larry said. Maybe.

There was a brief negotiation behind an odd sculpture next to a pretzel stand at the other end of the terminal. A cash bribe was exchanged. The Airline Agent's Supervisor started pushing buttons just to make it all go away. Somewhere on the internet, a seat became available and instantly was gone. And a deal was done.

A short shuttle ride later, Larry found himself at a bus station with a pocket full of money. He practically skipped up to the counter as the next bus was boarding.

To Larry at that moment, this seemed like the best thing in the world.

TEN - A COMPLICATED MATRICULATION

Under the streetlights outside the small apartment building not far from the diner, The Boy's car waits patiently, long past the middle of a deeply quiet night. A few stories above, The Girl rolls over beneath her open window and wraps her arms tight around The Boy. Her cat combs its ears on the sill, watching the rain and the Devil as he urinates on the car's front tire.

More than a year ago, The Boy's long-lost Uncle parked the car for the first time in front of the Paradise Diner, a late winter breeze twirling trash across the patchy asphalt. He handed The Boy the keys.

This'll be yours to, you know, get around in, his Uncle said.

Thanks, said The Boy, but barely heard him.

In a hospital across town, his Parents were dead and still holding hands.

The day they brought him home from the hospital, his Mother still worked at a cash register at the local department store downtown. His Father delivered the mail to their own neighborhood.

A photograph hung in the living room, from an afternoon The Boy always thought he could almost remember. The three of them in their little backyard. Bed sheet covered with toppling bowls of fruit and fried chicken. Empty wine bottle buried neck first in the grass nearby. Another bottle in his Father's hand. His Mother raising her own glass. The Boy's fists wrapped tight around their fingers as they helped his plump little body stand.

On the back of the photograph, his Mother wrote, *A Toast To Love.*

By the time he was seven, The Boy was the one cooking the dinners.

Running back and forth from the kitchen, he memorized complicated, nonsensical commands from his Mother, lying in bed. Her back hurt. She got headaches. A quart of gin on the bedside table.

The department store closed when the outlet mall opened up outside town, and she didn't like the new-fangled cash registers there.

After a while, he did the laundry too.

We don't deserve such a good boy, his Father always told him.

On his ninth birthday, the post office retired his Father early. Bad ankles, according to the forms. But they gave him chances and then gave him a choice. Always late. Too many afternoons stumbling through the neighborhood in a liquor cloud. Sudden bouts of the flu. They got by on half pay. Her family left them some money. The Boy picked up the yard duties too.

There was never fighting in the house. Never anger. Just an ever-present half-sleep. Comfortable darkness draping them off from the world. The Boy didn't know any different. If there was a ball game or school pageant, he found a ride with one of the other kids. Though school seemed nearly impossible, he never brought home a failing grade. Never once was there a phone call, a letter or even a note from his teachers. He sat in the back of the classroom and tried to blend into the coat closet. He never disturbed them. They liked to not be disturbed.

The day his seventh-grade school year ended, it occurred to The Boy that all might not be right with the world. After skipping home from the bus stop, a year of happy new memories bouncing along behind him. A year he grew four inches. Found a way to make new friends laugh. Stood his ground in a playground shoving match. The Boy's feet froze when he reached their front yard.

For the first time, he noticed the stale pallor of the house. Weeds left so long they became wooden trunks in random patches. The cracks and splits in the concrete walk. The curtains drawn tight. He felt the sweet scent of sweat and alcohol against his face. He didn't want to go in.

Well, hello there, his Mother said when he opened the door, setting her drink down among a half-dozen empty glasses. I've been waiting. Checkers?

The Boy stacked his papers and prizes on the stairs.

Sure, he said.

In high school, he found a place for himself outside their walls. Sports were never his thing, and no amount of effort made him a top student. But he found over time that people naturally like him. Like his smile. Listen when he has something to say. Though he rarely says anything. A lifetime of playing quietly alone made him thoughtful. Even tempered. Patient. He lived in two worlds. One where there might be a place for him. The other too complicated to explain. So he didn't. Just trudged off to school every day, his home life shut tightly behind a door in his mind.

There wasn't a time his Parents weren't together, quietly nodding off, day after day, year after year. Together they sat with him on the couch one Sunday afternoon, explaining the doctors would do anything they could. Together they made a quiet decision to call an ambulance on the morning of his high school graduation.

The Boy woke that day and groggily put on his suit, tucking his gown under his arm. Making his way downstairs, he looked himself over in the hallway mirror. Sleep in the corners of his eyes. The house still. Then, a patch of red light dragging itself down the wall behind him. An ambulance humming outside.

The nurses wheeled them into the same corner of the emergency room. After they hurried off, The Boy pushed the beds together. Holding hands, the three heard his Father's heart monitor drop into the eternal tone. His Mother quietly joined him.

I thought I might find you in here, said a voice at the hospital chapel door. An Uncle whom The Boy never knew.

Praying, he asks.

No, The Boy said. Just thinking. The door was open.

The first few days of work at the restaurant shoved past in a blur. It took a while for his mind to catch up.

For a long time before The Boy saw it, the Paradise Diner sat empty on its thin stretch of road. Thick with grime and grease on all sides. Rust eating an outline around the sign sinking into the roof.

His Uncle grinned as The Boy got out of the car and looked around.

So, this is the place, the Boy asked.

Yeah, what do you think, his Uncle asked.

Cool, I guess, the Boy said.

Fishing a fist full of keys from his pocket, his Uncle pushed open the door, and they began to work.

Inside, The Boy didn't know what to think as his Uncle fiddled around, elbow deep in a fuse box in the storeroom.

Alright, try it, his Uncle yelled.

The Boy flipped a switch behind the counter and streams of fluorescence collided with grime smeared across the row of dilapidated booths. He circled the counter. As he landed on a stool on the other side, stripped bolts snapped free. The Boy fell into the aisle with a thud.

When his Uncle found him lying on the floor next to the broken-off metal stool, they couldn't help but laugh.

Well, that's a place to start, The Boy said.

Soon, they found the grill entombed beneath ages worth of abandoned sludge. Generations of insects scattered when they pulled the grease trap. Same with the fryer. The best that could be said for the walk-in was it almost stayed cold. To the festering supplies abandoned there, it didn't matter.

They both took rooms at the efficiency motel down the road, The Boy not ready to go back to his house. Each morning, a knock came to his door just before the sunlight did. Each night, he dropped into bed, exhausted.

Sleep well, his Uncle said every time, but The Boy was always already dreaming. It was a week before he realized that he didn't know what the room looked like in the daylight.

With buckets full of any kind of cleaner, they swabbed tabletops, windows and the swinging door between the counter and the kitchen. At first just the top layers. Eventually, it was a matter of shine. One by one, they stripped down the jukebox selectors at each of the booths. With wet rags over their faces, the two struggled to pull one hunk of rotting filth from the walk-in refrigerator after another. It took elbow grease, wire brushes and at last a metal file to free the grill from its past. In The Boy's mind his Parents lingered all the time.

By week six, The Boy started on the floor. He already swept and mopped. Then swept and mopped again. But that day he started next to a booth on one side of the diner, got down on his knees and scrubbed.

In about ten hours, he made it fifteen feet, not even half the length of the counter. For a while before making him stop for the day, his Uncle sat and watched him smear his aggression into the floor. When The Boy finally collapsed into a heap, a distinct line showed where the floor was and where it was going.

Nice work, his Uncle said. We'll see how far you get

tomorrow.

Ok, The Boy said. Tomorrow.

A week later, they made themselves lunch on the now-sparkling grill, poured milkshakes and settled into a booth.

It was then, with warm gusts pouring through the propped-open front door and the smell of french fries in the air, that his Uncle explained he'd bought the place but didn't have the time to run it.

I don't understand, The Boy said.

I just need you to keep things moving, his Uncle said. I'll check in every couple weeks or send somebody to make sure everything's ok.

Why me, The Boy asked.

Things go well, someday it's all yours, he said.

But why me, The Boy asked again.

Because I believe in you, he said.

Oh, The Boy said. Alright, then. Thanks.

The cooking came easy to him. The constant cleaning like second nature. He loved conducting the beehive of activity. They hired Irene and the back-up Cook. Ordering supplies was no problem. He could predict very closely what they would need. The long hours didn't bother him.

It was keeping the books. Doing the math. Taxes. Time cards. All simply too much for him. The process, he understood. He got them done. But the whole thing took him forever and was exhausting.

After a few months, The Boy sat with his Uncle in the closet-sized office and asked for help. They'd been in there all afternoon. Naming sandwiches after street names and favorite customers. Debating the quality of various onion ring manufactures.

Look, I need more help around here, The Boy said.

I figured that, his Uncle said, sipping his coffee. I might have somebody.

Who, The Boy asked.

The night before, his Uncle sat in a coffee shop downtown, waiting for his newest waitress to walk through the door. She didn't know it yet. When the bell over the door chimed, he put down his newspaper.

Out, the Coffee Shop Manager barked at her. Go beg someplace else.

Screw you, it's cold, The Girl grumbled back.

Pulling off thin gloves, she waved crumpled dollars.

She's with me, The Boy's Uncle said. Coffee?

Whatever soup's on that sign out front, she said. Please. Hot.

ELEVEN - BIRTHDAYS AND BUTTERFLIES

On her sixth birthday, The Girl woke up to laughter. She padded to her bedroom door in footed pajamas. Her Mother giggled past in the hall. Her Father lunged with a pillowcase and ended up on his back at The Girl's feet.

Good morning, sweetheart. Happy Birthday.

I have it, her Mother said, and ran skipping to the back door, a butterfly cupped in her hands.

Her Father scooped The Girl into his arms and she squealed. When they reached the back door, her Mother was cross-legged on the lawn. Come on. Quick, quick. Here. Take a look.

Her Father sat her in his lap in the grass. Slowly, her Mother opened her hands. Gently, a huge blue butterfly stretched its wings. The Girl's eyes grew wide. She reached carefully toward the insect with one pudgy finger.

Careful, now. Careful.

The butterfly flapped its wings twice. But The Girl still didn't move. Hovering, the butterfly's panic subsided, and it landed softly on the back of The Girl's hand. As three faces pushed in tight, it explored her skin in a tiny circle for a long moment, raised its wings and flew away.

They dressed her for school and read the comics out loud while she ate her cereal. In an upstairs closet, her balloons and presents hid. She knew. They knew she knew. But nobody let on.

At the bus stop, they hugged her goodbye, and she started up the steps. Her Parents wrapped their arms around each other as she watched them start back to the house. The Girl waved. She never saw them again.

During recess, a Vice Principal strode solemnly onto the playground and pointed out The Girl to a teacher.

Tractor-trailer on the highway, she said. Rolled. They never had a chance. Poor dear.

The Girl didn't understand why a woman in a long gray suit took her to someone else's house for dinner. But she didn't ask. Just clutched her book bag in the back seat of the car as they drove out into the country.

Poor, poor dear, said a sweet woman at a farmhouse door. We'll take good care of her.

Still in her school clothes, The Girl passed through the door and stepped into a living room full of silent children. All in a row. Of all shapes and sizes.

Alright, introduce yourselves, the woman said. Then go eat. No screwing around.

One by one, eight of them filed quietly past her. Boys and girls. Big and small. Every size between. They timidly take seats at the table until one boy, younger but far larger than The Girl, drove his knuckles into her arm. The Girl dropped her book bag and screamed. The first sound she made in hours. A hand appeared, locked on the base of the boy's neck.

Move it, Warren, growled a much taller girl, just barely into her teens. When he moved on, she wiped at the smaller girl's eyes.

There now, she said.

Elizabeth, stop with that, the now-impatient woman said, piling dry potatoes onto the children's plates. Get over here. I'm not going to hear you complain there isn't enough.

That night, Elizabeth tucked The Girl into a top bunk in one corner of a room full of bunkbeds. Tears soaked her pillow.

Where's my Mommy, she asked.

You mind my Mother and you'll be alright, Elizabeth said. Since you're all Foster Kids, all she's allowed to do is yell. The state pays, but only if there's no trouble. So don't make any, and it'll be fine.

What's a floster kid, The Girl asked. Where's my Mommy?

Elizabeth's mouth twisted. Let's talk about it tomorrow, she said. Get yourself some sleep now.

The next morning, The Girl woke amid chaos. The shouting started early, rousting sleepy, belligerent children. Lines at the bathroom door and down the back steps to hang urine-soaked sheets. A giant, hairy, half-dressed man hovering among them. Kicks from the woman for anybody not awake. The Girl sat petrified, wide-eyed on her bunk, clutching her book bag in her arms.

Come on, Elizabeth said, dressing her in mismatched, badly fitting clothes, then planting her in a chair in the kitchen, in front of a bowl of cereal.

Keep your head down, Elizabeth said.

Dammit, Elizabeth, where's my coffee, Elizabeth's Father shouted, pounding his fist on the counter.

She walked over to a cabinet, drew out a pint bottle from the top shelf and poured into a dirty coffee cup. Her Mother's shrill voice suddenly echoing upstairs, Elizabeth runs to the rescue.

So, from there on, The Girl kept her head down. Torment from the other kids poured over her. Her precious book bag hanging from tree limbs. Sharp smacks when she wasn't looking. But all that stopped the second summer, after a fight with a kid named Jimmy.

Jimmy was almost exactly her age. He shoved her down the stairs, stole her seat on the bus, and told everybody she tried to show him her underwear.

Then he cornered her among the rusty, sharp-edged farm equipment. And told her how her Parents died.

Your Mom got crashed, Jimmy said. And your Dad. Crashed.

Shut up, she said.

No, he said. Your Parents got crashed by a great big truck. Into little pieces.

You don't know, The Girl said. You don't know anything at all.

Yes, I do, Jimmy said. I heard them talking. I know. I know more about you than you even do.

The rock balled in her hand struck Jimmy in the chest. He hit the ground hard. Screaming, The Girl landed on him, knees and fists first, punching and stomping anywhere she could reach as he pulled himself into a moaning ball.

When the other children appeared to cheer her on, she stopped. Jimmy in a lump at her feet, she glared at them, younger and older.

You all leave me alone, she said. We're all gonna have to start getting along around here. I mean it, now.

Warren sprints up to them out of breath.

They're hitting, he wheezed.

Nobody seemed surprised. Warren continued to gasp for breath. He struggled out his next word.

Elizabeth, he said.

All of them took off for the house, except Jimmy, blowing bloody snot bubbles in the dirt. The Girl stopped to help him up.

Come on, she said.

The kids hurried through the laundry room and found the dryer on its side. Broken plates and dishes scattered across the kitchen floor. Living room coffee table in a corner of the hall.

Elizabeth's Father had her by the hair in the front yard, a wallet full of money in his other hand. The children stood at frightened attention on the porch. Upstairs, Elizabeth's Mother threw her belongings out the window, cursing.

This one seems to think she can hold out on us, the huge man said. Thinks she can squirrel her work money away.

But we found it. We find everything. We know everything. So take a lesson.

Throwing her to the ground, he shoved the bills into his pocket, dropped the wallet and stomped into the house, children diving out of the way. The door slammed and the children worked quickly to gather Elizabeth's things. As she sat crumpled and weeping in the dirt, they quietly held them out to her. Elizabeth managed a smile.

Thank you, she said.

Get your asses in here, screamed Elizabeth's Mother from deep inside the dingy house. That one's dead to us. Last straw. Dead to us now. Dead to you. Get in here.

One by one, the children marched silently into the house.

That afternoon, the kids all retreated to different parts of the farm and waited for dinner. Down near the stream, The Girl found Jimmy looking for crayfish.

You ok, she asked.

Yeah, he said. I'm sorry.

Me too, she said. Your Parents. Did something happen?

No, they're coming back, Jimmy said. When things get a little better. When my Dad finds his job. Any day now. Soon. I just have to wait a little. That's all.

The house was back in order as the sun set. When the children returned for dinner, they moved slowly through the back door together, squeaking out the last bit of daylight. But something was in the air. Extra tense, like a violin string. Their macaroni and cheese was already on their plates next to burnt hamburger patties, long past cold. Elizabeth's Mother and Father sat at the table, angry, waiting. All by itself in the center of the table, a rusty lunchbox.

Oh no, Warren whimpered softly. No one else made a sound.

Every morning, the children marched a mile or so in any weather to meet their school bus. It's the stop for all the farms in the area.

On extra frigid days, the Other Kids' Parents sat with their children in the front of their pickups, warm and waiting for the bus to arrive. These Other Kids always stared smugly at the eight of them, shivering in cloth hand-me-down coats.

The Other Kids used to enjoy carefully noting stains and holes in whatever they wore. Then, on the previous first day of school, made a point of showing off all the new folders, rulers, pencils and pens their Parents bought them. This was the reason that at least one of these Parents now always hovered warily by, supervising, to keep their children from coming home with the same sort of bruises the Foster Kids shared.

Of all of it, day in and day out, this was the part that got to Warren the most. He called it, the not having.

Then one day, while digging beneath the seat of a junked truck in some corner of the farm, Warren found himself a lunchbox. Dented. Broken hinge. But he hid it in a hollow log near the bus stop and every morning carried it with him as he stood and waited for the bus. Empty. But something unto itself. Something for Warren.

Somebody thinks they're pretty smart, Elizabeth's Father said, nodding to the box at the center of the table. Everybody, sit down.

The kids sat and started eating.

Nobody said eat, Elizabeth's Mother barks.

You heard her, Elizabeth's Father said. Drop those forks. I was in the hardware store today and ran into the son of a bitch who owns the next farm over. And he tells me he thinks it's a genuine shame that we send a kid off to school with this rusty piece of crap. Couldn't remember which one of you had it. Or wouldn't say.

The children were like stone. Hands folded neatly in his lap, Warren quietly wet his pants.

Elizabeth's Father stood, grabbing the lunchbox with a hairy paw.

Let me ask it another way, he said. Line up.

The children swallowed hard and moved to their feet with the solidarity of dread. All together in a single motion. The Girl looked to Elizabeth's empty chair.

It's mine, The Girl said. I'm sorry.

Oh, you'll be sorry, Elizabeth's Father said, dragging her into the yard. Viciously beating her with the lunchbox. Carefully landing blows to keep the marks under her clothes.

Dragging her back inside, he tossed her into a heap in front of the children, still frozen at the table.

Take a lesson, he said.

Late that night, The Girl awoke stiff with pain. Circling her bunk, the other children watched her through the darkness.

I think she's awake, one of them said.

They'd slipped a cold towel onto her head, the way Elizabeth used to.

Thank you, said Warren, after the rest crawled into their beds.

Now a whole lot smaller than she, he stood watch over her for the rest of the night.

The Girl was on the road three years before The Boy's Uncle ran into her. Her travels began when Elizabeth's Father stood once again, in the front yard, this time before a new troop of frightened orphans. His fingers locked on The Girl's hair this time. The night before, she'd found him too near her bed for the last time. She left teeth marks on his arm that still flowed blood behind a duct-taped bandage.

This was not long after her fifteenth birthday. She knew she was born in the spring. She forgot the day. Roaming the streets, one city after another, with the rest of the unwashed and unwanted, they stole what they needed and begged for the rest.

She was the brave one who flirted with men outside of movie theaters and restaurants, then led them into an alley where her friends attacked, stealing anything they could grab.

She lived with a guy beneath an overpass, where he breathed paint and told her how much he loved her. One night someone pointed a gun at him and she shoved her own head in between. The next night he broke her nose with a brick as she slept. She ran as fast as she could as long as she could.

Then, along another cold highway, trucks and cars rushing past, The Girl extended her thumb into traffic, aggressive and battle worn.

In the distance, delivery truck taillights slowed. The Girl climbed into the truck cab where George waited.

Where you going, he asked.

The Girl was exhausted, hungry.

Anywhere but here, she said.

George drove without saying much for a while and stopped the truck outside a small coffee shop. He handed The Girl a few crumpled dollars.

Go on in there, he said. Try the soup. Trust me. It's good.

She took the money.

Thank you, she said.

Inside, the Boy's Uncle watched as The Girl ate her soup.

Heading anywhere in particular, he asked.

She groaned and tried to ignore him.

Not in particular, she said.

Need a job, he asked. Got any money?

Beat it, creep, she said, leaving.

Got a diner, he said. Need a waitress. Interested?

Halfway across the floor, she stopped.

I'm listening, she said.

Finish your soup first, he said. I've got time.

The day after they met The Girl, The Boy dropped his Uncle at the bus station in town with his uniform and hat.

This is your regular job, The Boy asked.

For the moment, he said. Wherever folks need to go. That's where I'm going.

The Girl rented her room and worked every day at the diner. The Boy said little as he prepared the food and handed it to her through the little window behind the counter.

Thank you, she said, each time the same way, eyeing him suspiciously.

Not a problem, he always answered, no matter what clever thing he thought up ahead of time to say.

One slow night, as he struggled with the books, the diner sat empty. Irene got bored and left early. The Girl slipped a quarter into the jukebox. She poked her head in the office door.

What're you doing, she asked.

Short answer, math, he said. Badly.

Here, she said. Let me.

Night after night, they spent those hours together in the tiny office. She told him of her after-work adventures. People she'd met. The bars. The bizarre house parties. The trouble and fun.

Each night he made his way back to his small room and thought of her as he drifted off to sleep.

You got to live, she'd say. Can't trust anybody. Got to have fun. Got to live. And he would always say, everybody's got to trust somebody.

He never followed her on her adventures into the night. Never tried to grope her as they stood inches from each other in the walk-in. He just promised to see her at work the next day and to looked forward to her stories.

Then one night, she didn't leave. She hung around with him as he shut done the grill, turned off the lights, and locked the door. They crossed the parking lot together.

Where's the party tonight, he asked.

Think I'll head home, take a bath, get some sleep, she said.

That's a little tame, he said.

She kissed him like a feather, turning toward town.

You're nice, you know that, she asked. See you tomorrow.

The Boy stood for a long time watching her walk through the parking lot lights. And then he slowly floated home.

Now, such a short time later, as the new couple sleeps beneath the moonlight, the Devil perches on The Girl's window sill, the giant black cat in his arms. In a few steps, he settles onto a chair across the room. With one hand, he pulls a pile of clothes from beneath him and tosses them on the floor. The cat squirms, but he holds it tight.

What do you think, he asks.

The big cat struggles in his arms.

Me too, he says. Me too.

The cat gives another futile twitch.

You know, I'm not bad, Satan says to the sleeping couple. Just evil.

They do not stir. He studies them for a long time as a cool breeze puddles their scents at his feet, then sighs.

With that, Satan fades. Sitting bolt upright, the cat now watches the couple with the Devil's eyes. It pads across the floor and up onto the bed. Nuzzling between their ears, the cat speaks gently into their dreams.

TWELVE - SOMEBODYBUYALADYADRINK?

The whine of asphalt slows as the bus reaches a filling station in some much-forgotten farming town. Outsiders find it charming. But the town itself never thought so.

Most of the Passengers jostle awake, squinting at the new day. The Bus Driver climbs out of his seat and stretches his legs at the bottom of the steps. The sun is bright in the sky.

The Reverend stands. Mitchell motions to Ernie.

This is our stop, he says.

Passengers trudge off the bus, stretching their backs in the street. Johnny is asleep, face smashed against a window. As is Albert, chin on his chest.

Silent and empty, the town stretches out alongside a dusty asphalt lane. Mitchell and Ernie follow the Reverend around to the rear of the bus, finding the Bus Driver latching the luggage bin.

Excuse me, but would you know where I could find a ladies room, the Reverend asks him.

That bar-and-grill looks open for breakfast, the Bus Driver says, pointing. Seems like the lights are on, at least.

I could sure use a drink, Ernie says as the Bus Driver turns back toward the bus.

Just another thing you'll have to learn to live without, so to speak, Mitchell says as they walk away.

Well, it is a little early, Ernie says.

Always five o'clock somewhere, the Bus Driver says over his shoulder with a chuckle.

All stop. The Reverend turns.

Excuse me, she asks.

Just thinking out loud, the Bus Driver smiles.

They watch him suspiciously for a moment, then shrug as they walk away.

Inside the bar, a handful of farmers nurse mid-morning coffee with the ham and egg special and a shot on the side. A room of quiet reflection.

The Reverend heads for the bathroom. Mitchell and Ernie find a table. Suddenly, a drunk Widow's voice booms, wall to wall.

Somebodybuyaladyadrink, she laughs.

The Bartender keeps on wiping the bar.

She peers around with one eye open, elbow on the rail, fingers tangled in a platinum wig, feet not quite touching the floor. She kicks at the top of an embroidered, fake mother-of-pearl purse tucked under her stool, the toes of expensive high heels stamped with rhinestone florets tapping against the wood paneling.

Goddamn never a gentleman, she mutters. The Local Guy next to her glances over, trying not to make eye contact. The Widow locks on him.

You married, buddy, she asks.

No ma'am, he says, setting down a cup of coffee and lifting his ball cap to itch his bald head with the brim.

Then how about a drink, she smiles. Good, me too. Hey, pal. One more for the kid and me.

He shrugs at the Bartender, who sets her up again.

Ma'am, if it's all the same, the Bartender says. Maybe you should . . .

Shut it, she says.

No, really, he says. Maybe . . .

Buddy, I said shut, she says. It.

Yes ma'am, he says.

The Local Guy steps off of his stool and sets a few dollars on the counter. When he pushes through the door, the outside world floods in. Along with all the other noise from the street is the long clang of a church bell.

The Widow's eyes rest on the face in the mirror past all the liquor bottles. Under all of the greens and reds and blues, so thick they don't clean off anymore, is a girl she used to know. She hated her freckles. Her long, thick, flat hair and dark, muddy eyes. She had eyebrows then, right where the looping and wobbly inked-on ones are now. She consults her drink, right down to the ice cubes.

She was a child in this town before the interstate, or much of anything else. The wind would always twist up that street outside the bar. That same short row of wooden false fronts. Past the dilapidated church. Such a long time ago. The road was dirt back then. Abandoned most of the day. Closing her eyes, she would lean into the swirling dust, as if it could lift her away.

This morning, the Widow is drinking again, despite certain promises. Her last husband freshly planted outside town. She didn't go. His family never liked her much. Never had a chance with that one.

Instead, she's thinking about the summer when the church bell rang and she stared down that road through town, watching the crowd file inside, waiting for the growing thunder of the Motorcycle Boy.

Crawling up behind him, roaring past the church, she wrapped her arms around his dirty-white T-shirt and smiled.

The Church Women, a gray-haired mass, squinting, snickering, gossiping their way up the narrow steps, lob their disgruntled attention her way. Young Deirdre smiling, pulling him tighter and tighter until their faces disappear into the cloud of the dust beneath that bike.

Her canyon-crossed eyes are now a picture-perfect match of her Mother's on those steps, carrying herself as if she never saw that bike go by. Failing to force the moment to pass. Tired.

Somebodybuyaladyadrink?

In a town built on hope and fickle, rocky ground, different doesn't hold up much. From her first toddling steps down those miles of dirt road, staring out across the flat and barren fields, anger filled in the empty spaces.

It's the same now in that barroom. Those same tractor cowboys. Same worn jeans, sneaking their morning beer and scuffing their boots. Every schoolmate read the bible before bed and hid cigarettes behind the barn. Mothers turned the light out early, tsking quietly together over coffee after their Husbands filled the fields. Year after year, season after season, forever bothered by rain or none at all.

Her best friend was anger. Anger because everything was the same and she was too. Anger because nobody cared, or didn't seem to. Never noticing the tedium of nothing moving through town but the wind and the dust.

She tried to tell them. Over dinner. After dinner. On and on about movie star magazines. Gossip. Major events. Anything else somewhere else.

Her Father gazed solemnly past her, chewing.

Then, something struck her. An idea like a freight train. So early on, she could never say when. From a feeling she always had. A sense she never could place. Faith in a savior lurking. There it was. All at once. Crystal clear. She waited and waited.

The promise of transients flooding the county every year to work the fields met her like a gust of wind before a storm. The ones barred from town until Saturday night, with good girls safely under key. They were there and they were leaving. They were the lucky ones.

Then her Parents noticed her interest. Her Father's long gaze turning mean and staying that way. They warned her. They wept. They shouted. They sang. They prayed on behalf of her innocence. Preyed on her doubts. Played up her fears. Shut her in. Shut her out. Too late. The wind whipping through her heart blew down a street someplace they'd never find her.

The Motorcycle Boy rolled into town on a Sunday afternoon that found her with ten or so town kids drinking pop outside the grocery, talking about looking for something to do.

He took them off-guard as they sat in the shade, flipping bottle tops. She was leaning against a wood post by the cooler, daydreaming. Never heard him coming. But there he was, with a roar, looking right at her. Too sudden to flinch. Air scattered. A combusting vibration ran through her.

She had on a long print dress that day, with sleeves falling from her shoulders. It never fit right. She wore that dress everywhere after that, thinking, as much as anything, that's what caught his eye.

He was tall and filthy around the edges. With fancy sunglasses. The kind airline pilots wear. Dark, dark glasses that never fit in when she tried to tell her friends that the first thing she noticed were his eyes. Yet she always, somehow, could remember them from that moment. Such a strange shade of blue.

The bike was road-worn and clanking a little. When he planted his foot, sound dropped with a thud all around them.

He cleared his throat and scratched at the rough skin on the back of his neck. Then, looking right through her, he said something dumb.

You dance, he asked.

All she could do was nod.

Stupid little girl, the Widow mutters to herself, kicking her feet beneath the barstool.

Well, all right then, he said, starting that bike, tearing out toward the fields and the men hiring for season work.

It was as if, she thought, shielding her eyes from the spitting dirt, that she was why he stayed. Why he didn't end up five towns over. Or a hundred. Because that's what free really is.

Who knows, mumbles the Widow into her glass. Maybe it was.

Nothing ever felt the same for her after that. From the instant the dust cleared, they all quietly stared. Including the Clerk who ran the register in the store, standing inside the tattered screen door that day, soon to be on the line with her Mother. After that, people tended to draw their own conclusions.

It was the next Saturday night, long after her Parents went to bed, that the Motorcycle Boy stumbled out of a dim, makeshift work-camp outside town and found her straddling his bike. Bare feet, chin in her hands, elbows on the handle bars, smiling. The moonlight turned that awkward dress to onion paper.

Remember me, she asked.

He did. She could tell. But he didn't say anything, just crawled on and together they took off.

They rolled out across those star-dripped fields. He shut off the headlight. She gazed endlessly into a sea of possibilities.

They kissed beside a fire in a rotten stump at the bottom of some dry creek bed. They did more than that. At least, he did.

When he slept, she put her head on his chest and stared up at tall clouds aiming arrows into the horizon. She could hear the enthusiastic applause of uncut crops waving goodbye.

Saturday night bled into Sunday morning and they

rolled down that single road through town together for the first time.

The racket brought people to their windows. That sure made her smile. They didn't understand her because they couldn't understand her. And now she was frankly none of their business.

Her Parents whipped her hard that night. And the Sunday after. And the one after that. All so worth it.

She would lean against her bedroom door, crying, laughing, as they piled furniture against the other side, forgetting the window.

How sad for you, she yelled through the keyhole, because she was the real kind of free.

Then word got around she's knocked up, or any variety of the vernacular, though, as it turns out, never actually a possibility, as physiology and irony would have it.

The Widow raps a fist of thick, shimmering rings against the bar, followed by a long rattle of bracelets gathered throughout her life. Trapped in one big house after another. Often finding herself sleepwalking toward that horizon, miles away from her big, soft bed and baubles. The landscaping and cars. The balding, flabby husbands snoring in fat chairs with scotch glasses in their laps. Jolting awake in the middle of some empty road. Out of breath. Half dressed. Even unconscious, she knew what she really wanted.

Fading Trophy Wife. Not an undistinguished profession or without its traditions. The Banker who shot himself. A Lawyer with a drug problem. An aspiring Con Man. The paranoid Industrialist. A clumsy Dentist. But first an aging Businessman, with a big car and no understanding of who she really is. Or was. Though, in his way, he was always very kind to her.

Each one was what bursts from the ground in a growing

county in a booming state. And somehow each one kept her here, in this one unforgiving place. She took their money, but couldn't bring herself to travel. Not under their steam. Barely done with one before the next one popped up. Like great, big rotting mushrooms on a nice lawn. Almost right before your eyes.

Eventually, her Parents stopped pounding at the door. A silence fell over the house. Like a blizzard hit on the inside.

Cold stares across the dinner table. Shouts stuck midair. Those sad, self-pitying faces, knowing, or thinking they knew, what was going on.

After that, she left through the front door. It rained for a couple weeks, so they would meet in the empty work sheds out in the fields. Or right in the middle of the street in the middle of town. But never at her house.

You don't understand, she told her Mother, who waited in a hard, wooden chair next to the front door, no matter the day or night.

It's not what you think, she repeated. They had plans.

The season ended in a month. He needed to learn these plans. So, one hot day, as they pointed the bike toward a pond in some field that felt a long way from the church bells, she figured it was time.

Let's swim, she said, grabbing his hand.

He pulled away and wiped down the bike with a pocket rag.

All right, hold on, he said.

She dipped her toe like those pinup girls, closing her eyes as she pulled off her dress and stepped in. Up to her waist, she reached behind for his hand, turned, and found him up the hill, under a tree, tipping his flask.

Well, she told her wide-eyed hangers-on as they gathered outside the grocery whenever she walked by. Mostly, we just talk a lot and sometimes you know, fool around a little.

Hey, she said to him as she stomped back to the tree. We should take off after the season . . . Hit the road . . . You know . . . Together.

He grabbed her by the arm and she smiled. Together, they rolled down the hill.

In a barroom fifty years and only a few miles away, this made the Widow bark out a thick laugh.

He looks so dangerous, one of the town's pretty little blondes once said to her.

She just giggled, twirling her hair.

That sort of laugh doesn't exist under the platinum wig. Just belts. Bounces. Batters. The whole place turns again to stare after the Widow lets a good one fly. Ernie, the Reverend, and Mitchell among them. She gives them all the finger and stifles a hiccup.

No, no, she lectured her classmates. He's sweet.

They'd trade blank stares.

He's really sort of a poet, she'd insist. And I trust him.

The Motorcycle Boy rolled her back toward the tree. The grass stung her thighs. It scared her. She shuddered. He liked that. His cold eyes never focused, ever, as long as she knew him. She thought it meant he could see the future. As if she wasn't even there, because he already knew her future self. A mark of real character.

He staggered over to the bike. So dangerous, she thought. So gentle. So perfect. She could already see them together on the open road. On that bike. Towns and highways in the distance. Her arms around him. Smothered in that deep, deep rumble under an open, open sky.

Somebodybuyaladyadrink?

The Widow slides from her stool. Her feet land heavy.
She scoops up her purse. Wobbles a little. Glares around.
And turns for the door.

The bar door flings open and carries her into the street.
The sun at her back, those church steps look so small now.

On the last day of the season that year, they headed once
more for the fields.

So, she said offhandedly, as if chatting about the
weather. When we leaving?

What, he asked, quicker than normal.

You know, leaving, she said. I thought, I mean, together.

Season ends tomorrow, he said. Got my pay.

He reached for his flask. She giggled and glowed. That
settles that. Full steam ahead. Leaving together made it all
just right. She smiled as they flew back toward her dumb,
old town. Just right.

And then in some new town. Down the road. Or some
city, maybe, or even a foreign capitol. Or Hollywood. When
they find the perfect spot. They'll settle down right there
and raise their family. She'll send home a postcard. That'll
show them all what's what.

The Motorcycle Boy dropped her off down the road
from her house and started away on his bike.

Tonight, she chirped as loud and as clear as she could.

He stopped the bike with a lurch and looked her up and
down. He smiled. She smiled. She went inside. Went
upstairs. Shoved her things into a bag she tucked under the
stairs. Mostly, she only had clothes. Including, again, that
uncomfortable dress she wore the first day they met. She
put that on. Then she waited.

The ancient Businessman at dinner that night was arched
like a dead tree. Owned a couple gas stations, or something.
With a huge face and sharp nose. He wore a linen suit and
held his hat when he shook her hand. Slowly, he bowed,

nothing on his scalp but sunspots and a few thin hairs.

She didn't touch her food. Just waited.

Then, as the rest of them politely finished dessert, thunder from the bike shook the front windows for the last time. She bolted from the table, family diving to catch her, far too slow. She flew through the front doors, abandoning the bag of clothes from her old life. Her Father shouting frantically after her.

A column of dust approached. She reached the road and threw her hands in the air.

The Widow tries to remember how he looked just then. Tries to focus on his face. But her mind just sees the jacket. The road pack hooked behind him. The black, steel-capped bike, snarling orange into the settling sun. The noise pounding toward her. The cloud that swallowed her as he passed her by and rolled away.

She stood in fresh, new, unfiltered silence for a long, long time. Then turned back toward the house. They crowded the porch and waited. Eyes all over her. Smug and consoling. Funny thing. Not long after that, she could never remember the guy's name. It disappeared into that mountain of field dust.

Alright, Deirdre, her Mother demanded. Enough's enough. Get back in this house.

The Businessman made an offer that night. Her Father took it. And when the passenger door slammed on the man's huge, shiny sedan, she waved goodbye with a faint smile. Thinking nothing at all.

Across from the bar, the bus starts with its own brand of rumble. Climbing onboard, the Widow trips up the steps, slides into the first seat and falls asleep as they cross out of town to join the highway flowing, finally, far away.

THIRTEEN - PENNIES FROM HELEN

After a forty-five-minute walk outside the tiny farming town, down a worn gravel road edged in long, stone walls, the Reverend, Ernie and Mitchell near a cute country house shaded by giant oak trees.

There, a chubby-faced man, walrus mustache flailing, shouts into a tiny phone sandwiched in his palm.

Yes, it's important, he says. None of your damn business. No, of course not. Yes. I'll be in when I get there. Excuse me?

The three stand behind him, watching quietly as the other caller hangs up first.

He pitches the phone to the ground. The ricochet leaves a mark on the quarter panel of his oversized blue sedan. His face is red. Sweat stands on his brow. It seeps at his suit-coat shoulder blades. Chasing down the plastic box, he scoops and throws toward a small patch of gravestones tucked into the woods across the road.

Mitchell doubles over, laughing. Ernie stares into the woods after the phone.

Now, now, the Reverend whispers.

The man spins to face them. He has a black eye and cuts along his chin. Purple, penny-sized welts cover his bald head.

Who the hell, he croaks. Oh, you must be, yes of course. How do you, how do you do, ma'am. Find everything alright? I'd have sent a car if I knew you'd be walking all this way by yourself.

He puts out his hand.

Walter, he smiles thinly.

Charmed, the Reverend says as they awkwardly shake.

The big man is smiling, but checking at his watch just the same.

Mind going ahead and, um, getting started doing, whatever that it is that you, you know, do, he says. My Sister suggested your, well, services. I'm not skeptical at all. I'd do just about anything to stop whatever it is that . . . I used to go to church, you know, and, um . . .

He keeps glancing uncomfortably at the house.

I'm a well-establish Real Estate Broker in this area, here you are, he says, reaching into his pocket to absently extend his business card with a practiced flourish. It doesn't do well to not be able to explain why . . . I just can't explain it.

He mechanically pokes at his welts.

Certainly, she says, moving toward the house.

Walter steps with her onto the lawn, freezes and leaps back. Additional sweat bursts across his forehead.

No, if it's all the same, he says, backing toward his car. No, I have a very important appointment in town with, uh, someone.

He circles the sedan and opens the door.

Dear, she asks.

Walter harrumphs, keys already in the ignition, then climbs back out of the car.

Ma'am, he asks.

My fee, dear, she says.

Yes, of course, he says, fishing a gold-trimmed, pre-inscribed check out of another pocket. He holds it out to her over the hood of the car. She doesn't budge from the yard, extending her palm. With a huff, the man rounds the car and leans from the road, out across the grass, to place it in her palm.

Thank you, dear, she says.

Just as he reaches the door handle of the car once again, Walter stops.

Ma'am, I do have one question, he says.

If your problem continues, simply stop payment, she says, tucking the check into her purse and turning her gaze toward the house. I'll give you ninety days.

Yes, of course, he says. Very reasonable.

With a puff of diesel, he disappears down the road.

You are just wicked, Mitchell laughs as they start across the lawn.

Hush, she says.

Though the storms from the night before passed, leaving deep, blue spots peeking from behind piles of stark, white clouds, a flowerpot full of rain rests against the front steps.

The unlocked door swings open, almost on its own. They step onto a round rug in the foyer. Dust dangles, painting the air in an otherwise spotless dining room. A crystal vase centering a small dinner table grips long-dead tulips. Rotting petals litter the hand-knit tablecloth. Picture frames holding children and others along the living room mantle bounce long sunlight squares. Newspapers and magazines cover an end table to one side of a doily-draped couch. A smiling ceramic woman with a large brass clock in her belly button holds a tall lampshade over her head in the corner.

Classy, Mitchell says.

Hush, the Reverend says. Will you keep Ernest company out front, please? I won't be long.

But, Mitchell begins to protest.

I'll call you if I need your help, she says.

But, he continues.

Go, she says. Please.

Fine, Mitchell says.

The Reverend tucks her purse under her arm and heads down the hallway toward the kitchen. Except for every fork and plate piled in the sink, this room is spotless as well, from the linoleum to the garden-print drapes. The Reverend finds the back stairs.

Pouting, Mitchell follows Ernie through the front door.

My Mother called me Ernest, Ernie says as they step outside.

Is that right, Mitchell says, plunking down next to the flowerpot on the front steps. You don't say.

It means honest, Ernie says.

Mitchell offers him a blank stare. A wafting breeze knocks a handful of acorns out of the trees. Ernie absently gathers them one by one.

I never thought it would be like this, Ernie says, throwing an acorn into the group of leaning, weathered stones across the road. Sure is a surprise. Do you think most people get surprised like this?

The next few, he aims at a tree with a long, whipping wind up.

Mitchell stares into the flowerpot with his arms folded.

I don't know, he says. Not much of a people person. Living people, anyway.

The dirty blue sedan creeps from behind the trees a little way down the road. Slouched in the front seat, the man with penny-sized welts peaks his fat forehead over the sill of the door. Unaware of the two watching him, his eyes scan the house. Reaching the point where the car rolls too far to crane his neck, he speeds off.

A breeze passes them by to find an upstairs window and flows across the Reverend's face at the far end of the upstairs hallway. She peeks into each of the rooms at the top of the stairs. In one, she finds the bedroom of a woman and a man, each with their various combs, jewelry and alarm clocks. Messy, with a large, lumpy bed. Another is a study strewn with books and papers jutting in every direction from a roll-top desk. The third is a guest room stacked to the ceiling with women's dresses, hat boxes and a collection of porcelain dolls.

Pushing open the bathroom door, the Reverend finds a tiny woman sitting on the edge of the tub, hands folded under her chin. She stares up at the Reverend with no urgency and little curiosity, sighing to herself.

Hello, dear, the Reverend says as the startled woman falls backward into the tub.

What, she asks.

Hello, says the Reverend.

The woman climbs to her feet, very, very confused.

Who are you, she asks. Can you . . .

I can see you, dear, the Reverend says.

And hear me, she asks.

Yes, I can, the Reverend says.

Well, the woman says, sitting down on the closed toilet seat. Doesn't that beat all?

The Reverend sits on the edge of the tub with her purse in her lap.

Tell me about it, the she says. I can help.

Who are you, the woman asks.

A friend, the Reverend says. What's your name, dear?

Helen, Helen says, shrugging. I'm Helen. And here I am, sitting in the bathroom. I'm not sure why. Nobody will listen to me. I'm not sure why. My Husband is an ass. That one's for sure.

Maybe start at the beginning, the Reverend says.

Tell you what, Helen says. I'll skip to the middle.

The sun is setting. Helen is in her tidy kitchen, busily working. Meatloaf in the oven. Grabbing a stack of bills from the counter, she notices the envelopes are missing stamps. Helen slaps her forehead.

The drapes flutter between Helen and the Reverend. Helen sighs again and stares out her bathroom window.

He sold my house, Helen says.

The Reverend watches her carefully.

Your house, she asks.

This house, Helen says. Knew I shouldn't have trusted him. But I did. Trust him. Then I'm in his den going through his desk one day, looking for stamps.

Helen rummages through Walter's roll-top desk. She finds a small stack of official-looking papers folded in half and hidden under the desk blotter.

Oh, Walter, Helen whispers through her normally polite teeth. You worthless bastard.

I find all this paperwork, Helen tells the Reverend. Though I didn't understand the particulars, I saw my address. My family address. This address. With *Sold* and some technical banker talk. Didn't take a genius to figure it out. I must be boring you, hon.

Not at all, the Reverend says.

Haven't had anyone to talk to, Helen says. At least anyone that listens. I was making meatloaf. Partly because it's easy, partly because that's all he seems to eat. And I had the oven heating when it struck me that I'd forgot to put all the stamps on the bills. But once I found all this going on, I marched right over to the phone and called him in his car. Because that's where he always is. His stupid car.

What did you say, the Reverend asks.

It's my house and he had no right at all to sell it, or even look at it funny, Helen says. Not without my permission. My Father built this house. My Mother gave it to me, and it's mine.

Of course, dear, the Reverend says. What happened after that?

I say to him, first thing in the morning I'm calling up a lawyer to straighten this out, Helen says. Then I took that oven dial and turned it up all the way. I said, I'll cook your dinner. Opened that door. Took that glass meatloaf dish in my hand and chucked it in as hard as I could. I thought it would break, you know? Shatter. Bang. But it didn't even crack. Just bounced around and tipped over. I sank down right there on the floor and bawled my eyes out.

The Reverend moves closer to smooth her hair.

But I picked myself up and headed up the stairs, Helen says. Threw everything of his I could get my hands on out the bedroom window. This went on for a while. Then a while more. And it got me winded. I closed the window. Sat down on the bed. I couldn't catch my breath. I think I might have slept there for a while, but I felt sick. Made it as far as the bathroom here. My heart beating so fast. That's all I remember. And then it was daytime. I woke up all curled up in the tub. No idea what happened. Or the time. Nothing. So I stand up and steady myself on the sink there. And from down the hall, here he comes with a box of my favorite hats.

Walter, the Reverend says.

Yes, and I say to him, you've got some nerve, Helen says. And he ignores me. Just walks into the spare room. And right behind him comes . . .

Helen stares at the floor.

Go on, the Reverend says.

Some little strumpet with one of my dresses in each hand, Helen says. She ignored me too. This was my Mother's house. She gave it to me. And next thing I know, there's some strange woman laying out her cloths on my bed. I think it's alright to be mad about something like that.

Certainly, the Reverend says.

Good, well, so then, here's my question, Helen says. Questions, really. How come no one pays any attention to me? How come, and this is the real weird thing, how come I can't so much as turn a doorknob? I can touch things, I can feel things, but I can't turn the TV on. I'm not hungry at all, and though I've spent weeks sitting right here in this bathroom, I haven't once had the notion to pee.

The Reverend smiles.

Tell me about the pennies, dear, she says.

Pennies, Helen says. Pennies I can do. Found one on the floor by the stairs and started fiddling with it. For some reason, small change is no problem for me. If you know why, I'd love to know too. So, I've been collecting coins. Nothing much else to do. It's amazing, no matter how much you clean a place, they're still everywhere. Lost in the couch, under chairs, everywhere. Plus, we have a great big jug of them in the attic. My Father dropped his pocket change in there every evening when he got home. Somehow or the other, I pushed it over.

Helen pats her pant leg. Her pocket jingles.

And you throw them at your Husband, the Reverend asks.

If he's going to move some tramp into my house, he gets what he gets, I'd say, Helen says.

And then, why in the shower, dear, the Reverend asks.

Helen shrugs her shoulders.

It's the only time I could get a good, clear shot, she says.

The Reverend laughs. She doesn't mean to. But she does.

Out front, the blue sedan again rolls past.

Yes, Mitchell says.

He'd sat silently for a while, staring at the sky through the trees.

Ernie chucks another acorn.

What, he asks.

Yes, Mitchell says. I think it does. Take everybody by surprise. If it surprised me, has to surprise everybody.

Oh, Ernie says.

They can buy it in their sleep or beneath the wheels of a freight train, Michell says. Doesn't matter. It's their expression. Genuinely a little shocked. It barely shows. Takes a skilled eye. But they all have that this-is-not-what-I-was-expecting look. Doesn't matter. We all get our mouths sewed shut sometime.

Frozen, Ernie eyes the pale man in the dark suit. Acorns drop from his hand.

Huh, he asks.

It's not all industrial strength rouge, Mitchell says. There can be certain unexpected mechanics involved in processing a corpse. Just what a soul will find to occupy its time post-mortem is a mystery to the living. A source of strain to the rest of us as well. But I tell you, the body isn't always ready to give up the fight. No, sir. They'll sit right up in the middle of their own wake. There's the normal physical reasons, sure. But I think, sometimes, they're just not ready yet. That one's awkward. The ten-minute intermission to wheel off somebody's relative to get his back broken, just to lay down flat for the sake of appearances. Not easy for anybody. Me included.

So you're, like, a funeral person, Ernie asks.

Mortician, Mitchell says. But I do try to put the fun back in funeral. That's a joke, of course.

You touch dead people, Ernie asks.

You are dead people, Mitchell says. So watch it.

Yeah, Ernie says. But . . . You touch dead people?

Mitchell rubs his forehead and groans.

Technically, I don't exist, he says. Why does my head ache?

Wow, Ernie says. I don't think I could handle that. I always feel creepy at funerals.

Well, I feel creepy in shopping malls, Mitchell says.

The sedan cruises past again. Ernie scratches his head.

What is with that guy, Ernie asks.

Something, Mitchell says. That's for sure.

Is that why you became a funeral guy, Ernie asks. Shopping malls?

Mortician, Michell says. No. My Father was. Is, actually.

That man will never retire. See, it all doesn't seem that gross to a kid whose summer job was holding the clamps while their Dad sawed through some tall guy's leg bone so he can fit into a standard-size box.

Ernie slumps.

You get the picture, Mitchell says. And I've never been well. Sickly is the word. Evidently. A fairly rare blood disorder. Broke down my liver. Kidneys. Then the asthma. Lungs pulling air. Absorbing none of it. An endless lack of oxygen made my face look like typing paper. My hair thinned. The other kids shied away. Partially through lack of fashion sense. There is nothing the matter with a well-tailored suit. Elementary school or not. But I was pale and bony. Weak and tired all the time. Combine that with the fact that my Dad had ten dead people in the basement at any given moment, it's not hard to see why I prefer those who are resigned to keeping their mouths shut.

Not me, Ernie says, again hunting the ground for acorns. At church, we have these big dinners and bingo. Dances sometimes. You ought to give one a try. Awful lot of fun. So you were sick?

Not everyone has the luxury of dying all at once, Mitchell says, counting quietly down from one hundred in his mind. The heart is beating, but after a while, you're not so sure what that means. Sometimes I wonder if I was ever alive at all.

Nine-year-old Mitchell watches his focused Father prepare a corpse. They both wear aprons over identical suits. Young Mitchell is wide-eyed and happy. The next moment, he stands amid a circle of taunting children, feigning dignity in his struggle to breathe.

Ernie, Mitchell says. Know the hardest thing to live with? Getting what you wish for. One afternoon, I was working on this nice young fellow who must have tried to race a train. Awful mess. It was a good deal of work, and I got tired. So I laid down on one of the metal tables for a nap. Not long after, I realize that I'm lying on satin. And not the fake stuff from the economy caskets. I'm in the super-deluxe. So I sit up, and there's Frank walking toward me. Frank is my assistant. Frank is an idiot. Was my assistant. Anyway. By the time I get to my feet, I see there's a guy in the box and he's wearing my suit. And then I was really pissed. Because that was a nine-thousand-dollar box and I'd left specific instructions, and I was very clear on this point, that I was to be buried in a plain pine box. It's such a waste otherwise. An expensive, ridiculous waste.

I think it's good to have nice, you know, that stuff, Ernie says.

I'm sure you do, Michell says. As I was saying, Frank is a moron. You have to tell him every little thing. And he wouldn't even look at me when I was yelling at him. Finally, I grabbed this big candelabra and pushed it right over onto the ground. Then this giant, awful vase. Out of frustration, really. See, at first at least, you can only move things around when you don't mean to. It's tricky.

Ernie looks down at the acorns in his hand. They fall to the ground at his feet.

Exactly, Mitchell says. Haven't really found the hang of it myself.

Flowers and lit candles hit the plush funeral home carpet. Frank screams. Mourners from another viewing come running. The Reverend is among them.

Now, now, everyone, Mitchell says. Show's over. Back to where you were.

None of them react to him. They comfort Frank.

It was like for a moment he was right here screaming at me again, Frank says. So horrible.

Well, up yours, Frank, Mitchell says.

Frank sobs. No one heard Mitchell, except the Reverend. She smiles.

Ernie watches Walter's car pass again.

Well, how are you doing now, Ernie asks.

Peaches, Mitchell says, standing to hunt for acorns. Never felt so good in my whole death.

Across the small road, hidden in a clump of trees on the other side of the gravestones, the Big Demon dressed in leather and the Little Demon dressed in wool watch Walter drive back and forth.

Schmuck, one says.

Complete schmuck, says the other.

Though just the two of them watched Walter all morning, lurking as he worked himself into a manic lather, suddenly they too are no longer alone.

Takes one, George says.

Georgie, the Big Demon says. How's it going?

Not so bad, George says. Yourselves?

Great, fantastic, the Little Demon says. Check this guy out.

The car slows near the house and speeds off again.

What about him, George asks.

One of these dumb, hot-shot realtor guys, the Little Demon says. Chamber of Commerce. Whatever. Big wheel around town. Real smart, he figures. Just waiting for his break. So one night, this guy walks up to him in a bar . . .

In a loud, crowded country bar, the Little Demon wears a grimy suit and slicked-back hair. Leaning in close, he has a drunk Walter's full and wide-eyed attention.

See, I'm Vice President of, you know, very heavy business, the Little Demon tells Walter. This is all confidential, you know. But I don't care. I'm one pissed-off person. See, the next Disneyland is going in just on the other side of your small and average-looking town. Very hush-hush. It'll be called, Disney Middle America. They'll start buying up the land soon. Cash by the barrel full. Name your price. Were I a fellow like you, I'd take them for everything you can get. Every dime. Greedy pricks. Take that to the bank!

The Little Demon staggers away. The gears are turning behind Walter's glassy, bloodshot eyes.

Nice one, George says.

Yep, the Big Demon says. Next thing we know, he's borrowing money from anybody willing to take the time to break his legs.

In a cramped, empty storehouse basement, a cross-eyed, rural Loan Shark pushes a briefcase across a table to Walter, studying him suspiciously.

I hope for your sake you know what you're doing, Walter, he says.

Walter anxiously grabs the case and winks.

Don't you worry about me, he says. I'm just making a few investments.

And he came close, real close, to raising enough cash to buy up all of that land, the Big Demon laughs. Worthless lots. Strip-mined to hell. Half of it junkyards where folks dump who-knows-what. But a couple of them hated to sell. So he upped the offers, two and three times over. Still a deal with Mickey on the way.

Walter and a shirtless Farmer stand in a scrub-covered field. They lean over the hood of a pickup truck to sign a stack of papers.

Mind you, I'm practically throwing in all the scrap metal

for free, the Farmer says.

Yes, yes, Walter says. Just sign on the line.

Right, the Little Demon says. So he's still a little short on the money. Doesn't know what to do. Right? But then he realizes this house here was worth just about enough. Nice little house. Not hard to find a buyer.

And what about his Wife, George asks.

What about her, the Big Demon asks.

Didn't she own the house, George asks.

The Demons wonder why he knows this.

As a matter of fact, the Big Demon says.

What's a forged signature or two between family, the Little Demon says. A minor distraction when there's millions, maybe the start of billions on the line. Car dealerships. Miles of them. That's his real scheme. A whole state covered in low-priced imports. That's the big dream. Then he could buy it back for her. Buy ten of them if she wants. A hundred. Simple.

Simple, George says.

A two-minute conversation with the guy, the Big Demon says. Hasn't been a time yet when we didn't just suggest what they wanted to do anyway.

As the sun sets on Walter and the Farmer, rain clouds roll in. The Farmer squints endlessly at the contract. Walter's phone rings.

Helen glares at her kitchen phone receiver, her home's proof of sale balled in her other hand.

Damn you, Walter, she yells.

So when she finds out, he panics, the Big Demon says. Even though she still didn't know the first thing about the big picture. Plan was, he'd head for Barbados with this little Co-worker he's been seeing and explain it all from there.

But the whole thing hinged on the money from that house.

Tiny raindrops on his windshield, Walter squeezes the wheel. Trees fly by. Night is falling. Helen is still on the phone.

I'm getting a lawyer, Walter, Helen shouts through the cracking phone speaker. A lawyer! You hear that?

This next part is the great part, the Little Demon says.

Yes, it is, the Big Demon says. And just goes to show that we're not the bad guys here. We just embrace ambitions not addressed by today's public school systems.

George laughs.

Maybe so, he says.

Helen angrily flings Walter's things around their bedroom.

Walter sneaks in the back door and hears Helen's commotion upstairs. He spies the stove.

Helen has no idea he's in the house. She slams the window shut and collapses on the bed, out of breath.

Walter opens the oven and sees the meatloaf. He blows out the pilot light, then turns on and blows out each of the burners for good measure. Gas seeps up the back stairs.

A stroke of genius, the Little Demon says. One big boom and his problems are over, right? House insurance takes care of everything. Life insurance policy to boot. But no boom.

In the dining room, Walter lights the dinner candles with silent relief. He skips softly across the kitchen. And with his usual flourish, pulls the back door shut behind him. Which blows the candles out.

Helen stumbles into the bathroom, disoriented. She

stares into the mirror. Struggles to catch her breath. Tears standing out in her eyes.

A rural route Mail Carrier steps to the front door and finds the letter box empty. She smells gas. She knocks.

Frosted glass breaks beside the door. The Mail Carrier's arm emerges and gropes for the lock. She turns off the stove. Covering her mouth, she throws open the back door.

Then she finds Helen sprawled across the bathroom floor. Blood trickles down her face and also the edge of the sink, from where she passed out and hit her head.

She'd been dead a while, the Big Demon says.

Congratulations, George says.

Oh, now, come on, don't be like that, the Little Demon says. We didn't do it. He did.

Truly, the Big Demon says. At first the guilt just crippled him. But the cops didn't seem to care and his new lady friend moved in. After that, all he had to do was wait for the sale to go through.

Walter's Girlfriend unpacks her suitcase onto Helen's bed. She and Walter embrace. Helen stands in the doorway, furious.

Later, Helen sits at the top of the stairs and absently fiddles with a penny. Realizing what she's doing, she picks it up.

A smiling Walter steps into a running shower. He pulls the curtain closed. Helen steps into the bathroom, her pockets jangling with pennies. Coins ricochet across porcelain and tile. Walter screams.

Then it happens again the next day, the Little Demon says. And again the next. He's losing his freaking mind. What are we supposed to do? Not love our job?

George pushes past them, heading toward the house.

Oh, don't go away mad, the Big Demon says.

They chuckle, hiding their concern.

George crosses the road to find Ernie and Mitchell gathering acorns.

Hello there, George says.

They are shocked to be seen.

Reverend inside, George asks.

They nod.

Thanks, George says and strides into the house.

Who was that, Ernie asks.

Haven't the faintest idea, Mitchell says.

George finds his way to the kitchen and up the back stairs. The sound of women laughing draws him down the hall. He gently pushes open the bathroom door.

My goodness, George, the Reverend says. What are you doing here?

Just in the neighborhood, he says. Hello, Helen, how's things?

Lousy, stranger, Helen says. Yourself?

George smiles.

I think I can clear some things up for you, he says. By your leave, of course, ma'am.

Certainly, the Reverend says.

Terrific, George says. Follow me.

Together, they descend the stairs.

Can I get you some tea, or, Helen stops, wobbling for a moment, her bottom lip quivering. Oh, I guess not. This is all too much.

The Reverend takes her by the elbow. They cross the foyer. Helen stops at the front door.

It's alright, the Reverend says, and together they step out into the yard.

At the sight of Helen, Ernie tucks in his shirt.

This is George, the Reverend says to them. He's an old friend. This is Helen. This is her house. George, Helen, this is Ernest and Mr. Mitchell.

I've heard a lot about you, George says to Mitchell, then turns to Ernie. Sorting things out alright?

Sure, I guess, Ernie says.

Tell you what, George says. I need to chat a minute with the Reverend. Can you guys meet us over across the road?

They nod, moving quickly. The Reverend squares her shoulders.

What's on your mind, George, she asks.

Hard to find the words, George says.

You came a long way, the Reverend says. What is it?

Think there were ever real dragons, he asks.

Dragons, she asks.

Big crocodiles, he says. Wings. Fire.

I know what a dragon is, she says. And no. Not that I've thought about it. Maybe. Why?

Mesopotamians, George says. Four thousand years ago. They had this goddess. A dragon. Or close. Lived in the ocean. Had to kill her to have a proper universe. That was the idea. Back then. After that, the Romans and Greeks went for dragons every time. Fierce. The best. And if you can conquer the best, then you are the best. On their shields, on their boats, on their flags. Everywhere. Dragons.

The Reverend settles down on the steps, her bible beside her.

You know, I was a soldier once, George says.

I know, the Reverend says.

A good soldier, he says. A good citizen. Very bold. Which I thought made me strong. But not just physically. Convictions. That's what mattered to me. Such strong convictions. I kept them like children and counted them every day. The only important dragon to me was the picture of myself in my mind.

George picks up the Reverend's bible and flips absently though the pages.

He was dead two centuries by the time I heard of him, George says. I had no reason to think any different from everybody else. My friends and my family, myself, we called those people ridiculous. At best. Disruptive. That's what all good Romans thought about idiots ranting on street corners, making up stories. But I stopped more and more. I listened. Eventually, I stood up for what I'd come to believe. I began to speak on my own. So a crowd threw rocks at my skull. Broke my bones. Spit. Cursed. And as blood poured into my eyes and as I died, it all made sense. So fitting that they could beat the dragon's body, but they couldn't touch his heart.

Across the road, Helen, Mitchell and Ernie pretend not to look, waiting intently for what happens next.

But something occurred to me recently, George says. These days, people have their own ideas about dragons. In the artwork they get trampled under the feet of whichever Martyrs and Saints. The defeat of the pagan hordes. That story about me. A town feeding some girl to a dragon. As a sacrifice. To protect their sheep or something. I ride up and wrestle it to the ground. Use her corset as a leash. Very sexy. And home she goes, leading it as gentle as a puppy. But I've never seen a dragon.

George snaps the bible shut and hands it back to the Reverend.

Born a Roman, died a Christian, he says. Sometimes I stare up at those stained-glass pictures and wonder if I'm trampling myself. Who knew it would be like this? Not me.

What brings you here today, George, the Reverend asks.

Got this thing to do, George says. Involves these kids and the future of just about everything. Not sure if it's right. Or wrong.

The Reverend holds out her bible with both hands.

You know why I read this book, she asks. I mean, there are other books. Lots of them.

Why, he asks.

Because I'm only one person and I know it, she says. Every moment of every day, I do the best I can. But I can only do so much. Everybody can only do so much. And if there's one thing for sure, it's that there is a lot more going on out there than I'll ever understand or even know about. So, every day I do my best. I make the choices that are right for me. For the rest, I trust the book.

George stands, listening long after she stops talking.

Thanks, he says. That'll help.

My pleasure, she says.

Across the road, Ernie whispers loudly to Mitchell.

Don't look, he says. Who are they?

I said I don't know, Mitchell says.

The Big Demon and the Little Demon grin at them through the bushes on the other side of the grave markers. Snarling and laughing. Joking around.

Don't mind them, George says, crossing the road with the Reverend. They're worthless. And harmless. Mostly worthless. Hey there, Helen?

Helen leans against a headstone, lost in thought. She snaps out of a long stare.

Yes, she asks.

I'm not sure how to tell you this, George says, nodding toward the stone beneath her.

Reading, she staggers, catching the Reverend's shoulder, laughing and crying all at once.

He didn't even put me in a real cemetery, Helen says. Can you believe that? He wouldn't even bury our cat over here.

Walter's car appears once again, cruising past the house. The big man leans away from them across the passenger seat, staring into the front windows. Frantic.

Walter, Helen shouts. Dammit, Walter, what did you do with my burial plot? The one near my Grandmother. What did you do, sell it?

Walter's neck and shoulders stiffen. He freezes at the wheel. Then, all at once, he pivots toward the sound of his Wife's voice. Eyes goggled, he chokes. There he sees the Reverend and Helen, standing together among the stones.

His palms curl around the top of the halfway open driver-side window. The car speeds up and lurches off the road. Walter glances down at the wheel as if seeing it for the first time. He stomps for the brake. Misses. The engine roars. The doomed sedan buries itself into an oak tree in the front yard with a thunder crack of bending metal.

Airbag deployed, Walter rolls from the car and drags himself onto his feet. Tearing at the knot in his tie, he staggers toward them.

Helen, he cries. Thank the Lord! My darling! It's so good to see you . . .

Walter stumbles, lunging. His legs buckle as he grabs at his chest. He ends up on his back in front of them, his last living expression, puzzlement over where all these other people came from.

Fudge you, Walter, Helen says. Double fudge.

Giggling, the two Demons prance past George.

'Scuse us, the Little Demon says.

Shall not kill, George says.

Shall bite my ass, the Big Demon says.

Ma'am, the Little Demon says as they pass the Reverend.

Ma'am, the Big Demon says.

She ignores them.

They lean over Walter, hot breath inches from his face.

Wakey, wakey, the Big Demon says.

Walter sits up, quivering and startled. They pull him to his feet. Disoriented, he turns first to the Reverend.

Ah, hello, he says. Real quick, while I'm thinking of it, if I could get a receipt . . . Helen, oh, Helen, hello, I . . .

His head swivels. Then Walter notices his own body

lying at his feet, squeals and faints. The two Demons drag him toward the woods.

See you around, Georgie, the Little Demon says.

Both Demons explode with laughter as they fade into the trees, Walter now screaming bloody murder.

Ernie's worried.

Where are they taking him, he asks.

Oh, George says. He'll realize the error of his ways. But on a lighter note, you guys are coming with me.

Wait, Mitchell jolts. Who is?

Not you, George says.

Why, Mitchell pouts. Why them?

Don't ask me, I just work here, George says. Helen, Ernest. Come with me and you can get a little more acquainted. Reverend, I . . .

I'll see you around, George, she says. You take care.

Yeah, George says. Thanks again.

Helen takes Ernie's hand as they walk together.

You know, Ernest means honest, she says.

Ernie grows a huge grin as the three quietly fade into the trees.

Balls, Mitchell says.

Watch your mouth, a voice near them tones.

Hello, the Reverend squeaks.

Mary and Morgan now stand nearby.

Hello, Mary says.

Hi, Morgan says.

This is quite a day, the Reverend says. Quite a day.

Hello to you, Mitchell says. Whoever you are. But if I can beg your pardon a minute, Reverend, this isn't fair. It isn't, you know? I mean, what is it I have left to do here, anyway?

Excellent question, Mary says. Listen a moment.

Listen, he asks.

The sound of Lost Children talking and laughing tumbles from the woods like a gust of wind. It stops. Then flows again as a hundred small faces peek from the leaves. Tiny bodies rise from bushes and drop from tree limbs. They gather around the clearing full of tombstones.

Mary kneels to look Morgan in the eye.

Watch over them for me, she says. I'll come get you when I need you. This won't be easy. Yours is a heavy price to pay, young lady. Plus, you'll have to deal with this guy.

I don't understand, Mitchell says.

Everyone deserves a childhood, Mary says. But not everyone gets one. Do they, Mr. Mitchell?

As they move closer, scars appear across some of the Children's faces. Others are bald and thin. More seem twisted, as if bent by some great force. But now they are free of their pain. Smiling. Eyes dancing.

Wait, Mitchell says.

Slowly, the Children gather around them and lead Morgan and Mitchell toward the trees, already laughing and playing again. Mitchell looks to the Reverend with a question mark on his face.

I'm not ready, Mitchell says.

Go on now, the Reverend says. And do watch your language.

The group disappears as quickly as it arrived, leaving Mary and the Reverend alone in the clearing.

Looks like something's on your mind, the Reverend says.

I'm having a tough time, Mary says.

Just love them, the Reverend says after a long moment. That's all they need, if you're asking me. Nothing more than that.

FOURTEEN - SOME DAYS

George spends the rest of the morning alone in the parking lot of the Paradise Diner. Staring at the building. Pacing back and forth.

Inside, The Boy is crammed in his closet-sized office with the local police.

From just after dawn, black and white cars sat cooling outside. An ambulance quietly arrived to load Ernie's body, then move slowly back down the road. Later, they hauled off his widowed rig. For the longest time, the green-faced man in the hunting vest mumbled woefully in the back of a cruiser. Officers took pity. Eventually, they sat him down with some coffee at a booth on the other side of the diner, in full sight of the blood stain stretched across the floor.

Someone already asked me all of this, The Boy says to the Police Officers crammed into the little space on the other side of his cluttered desk.

Just a few more, an Officer says. So, to be clear, his place belongs to a relative?

Yes, The Boy says. My Uncle.

And you run it, the Officer asks.

Yes, The Boy says.

And you are how old, the Officer asks.

Nineteen, The Boy says.

And this Uncle of your's is where now, the Officer asks.

He travels, The Boy says.

And you run this whole place for him, the Officer asks.

When he's out of town, The Boy says. Yes.

So, then, where is he now, the Officer asks.

Traveling, The Boy says, losing his patience a little. Go ask anybody. Seriously. Please.

Alright, alright, the Officer says. But we want to talk to him as soon as possible. Understand?

Sure, The Boy says. Of course.

After they all leave, The Boy stares at the bullet hole in the window for a long time, then finds a bucket and some gloves to start cleaning.

It's going to be a weird day, he mutters to himself.

The Boy woke early, like every morning. But this time he awoke in the arms of The Girl. So he soaked that moment in before heading for the diner. His mind drifts there again as the mess around the booth seems to get bigger.

Yet, the warm blankets he settled into the night before felt less comforting as daylight arrived. Not so soft or safe. Sometime before dawn, he began to toss and turn. His skin tired and not a part of him.

Trying to concentrate on the day ahead as he drove over to the diner, his mind frantically searched for something he couldn't name. An echo of sensation passed over him at times and an emptiness hovered, fidgeting at the back of his neck.

The Boy throws his dirty rags into the goo and stands. Stretching his legs, he wrinkles his brow. All morning, a picture sporadically locked in his mind for just moments at a time. The same sort of thought as when looking for his car keys.

Closing his eyes, The Boy sees it again. In a dark corner, beneath a thick curve of metal, sits a small, weathered, brown leather satchel. Blinking, he thinks about another cup of coffee and the blood on the floor. Then the satchel again. He shakes his head and gets back to work.

The Girl wakes with the same strange feelings and the cat curled against her. There is a brand new emptiness in a place she can't quite find and a faint, drifting memory of bliss. She spends the longest time lying there. Eyelids closed. Mind floating around the room. Such an odd dream.

As The Boy wipes the last trace of blood from the floor, George lets go of a heavy breath, puts his hands on his hips and kicks a stone at his feet.

Not in much of a hurry, Jesus says, now standing beside George in the parking lot.

Without glancing over, George shrugs. Not sure what I am, exactly.

You're my friend, Jesus says. And I need you to do this thing for me.

I don't understand, George says. How do I warn them without telling them? And why? I can't see why.

Remind them how much people have to lose these days, Jesus says. And don't tell me up to this point it's all been pretty.

George glares at the diner.

Let me tell you something, Jesus says. Nobody likes a tourist.

It's the same thing over and over, George says.

They all get their own shot at it, Jesus says. That's all.

Give me a second, George says.

From a clump of trees beside the building, The Girl appears in full stride. She heads for the back door.

Go on, get in there, Jesus says. It's you for a reason. I mean, think about it. What's the biggest danger facing kids like that these days? Sure isn't us. Not by a long shot.

Yeah, George says. I suppose so.

He doesn't need to turn to know Jesus is gone.

Inside the diner, The Boy hears the back door slam shut.

Hey, The Girl says, throwing her books on the counter. What's up?

He tells her all about the blood.

The police are looking for Irene, he says.

She's probably curled up in her Mother's attic getting drunk, The Girl says. She does that. I don't blame her.

Yeah, The Boy says, absently wiping the counter.

What's wrong, she asks.

Got this feeling like I'm missing something, he says. You seen, like, I don't know, like a little leather bag? I don't know how else to describe it.

Something clicks. The Girl grabs his hand and pulls him through the kitchen door.

They pass the grill and the fryer. She pushes through the back door. When they get to the dumpster, she closes her eyes and holds out her hands, searching for the picture in her mind. The Boy is already on his stomach in the dirt, fishing below the giant metal garbage can. Pulling out the worn leather bag, he holds it between them.

I had a dream about this last night, he says.

Yeah, I did too, she says, grabbing it from his hands and rushing back into the kitchen.

On a long metal table used to cut vegetables, she removes a small vial and two syringes.

What is it, he asks.

Heroin, she says.

How do you know, he asks.

I knew a guy, she says, and leaves it at that.

The Boy is concerned.

Did you, he asks. Try it, I mean.

Never enough to share, she says. But he'd lie on the floor and tell me flowers were growing out of his chest.

Sounds like this dream I had, The Boy says. All morning I felt bits of it washing over me. Something just like that. Not all the time. Only every once in a while.

The Girl turns the vial in her fingers.

Weird, she says.

The bell over the front door rings.

George steps into the diner.

Hello, he asks the empty room.

There is a commotion in the kitchen. The Boy and Girl emerge, blushing and without the bag.

Am I glad to see you, The Boy says.

The Girl stares George up and down.

Do I know you, she asks.

This is George, The Boy says. Friend of my Uncle's.

The Boy hands George a police report. He looks it over.

The things that happen to people, George says.

You can say that again, The Boy says. They're going to want to talk to him.

I expect so, George says. I'll let him know.

The Girl is trying to place where she's seen George before.

Want some breakfast, she asks.

Yeah, George says. The Special. Thanks.

Hey, George is a smart guy, The Boy says, heading for the kitchen. Ask him that thing from your school.

She pours George a cup of coffee.

He picks it up.

What thing, he asks.

Oh, this stupid essay I got to write, she says. Community college near here. It's on the application.

Alright, he says. Go on. What is it?

Name the greatest danger facing kids today, she says. You can see that written on a chalkboard, can't you? I'm tired of thinking about it.

The cup stops short of George's lips. He sets it down.

Too hot, she asks.

Coffee's fine, he says. What do you have in mind?

No idea, she says. Whatever they want to hear. Premarital sex? Credit cards? Don't screw. Don't spend. That's the normal stuff, right? Never throw a rock at a cop car? Something they can sink their pointy teeth into. Nobody wants a real answer.

What's a real answer, he asks.

Life, she says. That's the big one.

Life, he asks.

I see life kick people in the ass on a regular basis, she says. Don't you?

You mean, why do bad things happen to good people, he says.

No, she says. I mean, why do good things happen to bad people?

The Boy emerges from the kitchen.

That poor dead guy wasn't hurting anybody, he says. Bad luck, that's all.

I heard some magician say once that luck's just chance taken personally, she says.

George finds the sugar.

That so, he asks.

World fires enough bullets, going to hit somebody, she says.

So, then, what do you do, George asks. Fire back?

Used to, she says. Not lately.

The kids are both grinning a little. A flickering moment of relationship takes a first public trial run before George's eyes.

Right, George says. So where does that leave you?

I'd say with just enough rope to hang ourselves, The Girl says.

I'd say so, George says and stands to leave.

What about breakfast, The Boy asks.

Have it here the next time I walk through this door, George says, and then he's gone.

What was that, The Girl asks.

Strange, The Boy says. Strange damn day.

After George leaves and all throughout the afternoon, business is dead at the Paradise Diner. Around noon, a regular customer, a Barber from the town, comes in to settle a bill from the day before.

Everybody's still busy talking this and that about your little incident out here last night, he tells The Boy. You know how people are. They're spooked.

Yeah, The Boy says, his thoughts still circling the small vial of powder hidden in the worn, leather satchel behind a pickle barrel in the storeroom.

Not to worry, people forget, it'll pass, the Barber says, and has his lunch somewhere else just the same.

The Boy hangs a closed sign on the door and looks over at The Girl, sitting in a booth, staring out the diner window, a dreamy look in her eye. He sits down across from her.

She starts to say something and stops. He does too. Then, together, they charge toward the storeroom, digging out the leather satchel and spreading its contents across the floor.

I can't get this out of my mind, she says.

Me neither, he says.

We should dump it down the toilet, she says.

Yeah, he says.

But neither moves.

Outside the diner, the Devil places his palms on the thin metal wall separating him from The Boy and The Girl.

Think hard, he flitters into the back of their minds.

Seemed like scary stuff in health class, The Boy says.

I don't remember much from health class, The Girl says. But I've seen some people pretty strung out. I knew one lady who sold her kid to some guy. Or, I guess, rented, you know. After she lost her house, her car, everything. Crazy to think something could be that amazing that you would give up everything for it. But . . . Just once . . .

. . . couldn't hurt just once, he says. Could it?

A long moment passes between the fry cook, the waitress, and the happy devil outside.

Might as well try everything once, they all agree.

Satan leans back against the diner and smiles wide.

Meanwhile, the rain that fell in the hours before left clouds as tall as mountains hanging heavy over fields the bus now crosses. Too tired to pour anymore, they trudge toward the horizon. Acres of weeds reach back toward the sky, shaking off their damp morning. They find the sun as Jack Eddy puts down his ink-covered notebook. Eyelids drooping, he stares wearily out the window.

Near the intersection of two empty roads, the bus passes a small, open space cupped in a horseshoe of tall trees. Albert balances his hands on his cane and rises to his feet.

Stop here, please, Albert tells the Bus Driver.

What, the Bus Driver asks.

Please, pull off the road, Albert says.

You alright, the Bus Driver asks.

Yes, Albert says. Just please, please pull over.

The bus slows. Passengers rock forward in their seats, raising their heads to break long highway trances. Albert patiently toes the white line at the top of the bus steps and disappears through the parting doors.

At first no one else moves. Through the windows, they watch Albert slog across the mud and grass, his cane vaulting him along.

Albert's mind is far away, near a small lagoon on the gulf side of Florida. Light slipping beneath the swamp flowers sparks a buzzing neon sign for the Meridian Inn. No one else around. No one in the world. Except his delighted young Wife, finding her suitcase, her bathing suit, the powder-white sand and water. A cheap bottle of champagne and jagged ice in the sink. Gravel under his deck shoes. Bugs everywhere. Closing his eyes. Feeling her near. Growing darkness.

The Bus Driver takes off after Albert. The Passengers stretch their legs, filing off of the bus.

But Albert's in the suburbs. She and he move a hand-me-down crib through the front door of a small brick house. A couch. An ugly, ugly lamp. Dirt gives way to a struggling lawn and the handfuls of dandy lions she pulls, week after week, for what was supposed to be forever. Her smiling. Her caring. Albert watching her watching their family sleep. Softly singing. The picture's there but the song is gone, muddled into a million others.

Tears flow to Albert's eyes. Blinking them away, he stops. Catching up, the Bus Driver stands with him there, listening.

Ever see a guy pull a plow all on his own, Albert asks.

Don't think so, the Bus Driver says. You?

Once, Albert says, pointing his cane. From way over there by those trees to past here where we're standing. Never seen that much effort come out of a person. Before or since.

Wind sweeps the empty patch of ground. Fully disembarked, the Passengers group in the dirt at the edge of the road, holding the sun from their eyes and guessing at the situation.

There was a bit of a farm here then, Albert says. Not much of one. Right after the Army, I stopped through here on my way back home. There was this big party going on. Big get-together. People from all over these parts. One of those warm summer afternoons when the air sort of glistens. My uniform was the only clothes I had. Everything else in a duffle bag. I could feel freedom in my fingertips. Safe and sound. Young. Strong. And that day was just splendid. Lovely, with meat cooking. Beer cold like ice. And these fellas, I guess they worked on the railroad, were betting on how far somebody could pull this plow rusting in the mud. Well, it wasn't going to be me. They all start shouting for Roscoe. Roscoe. Everybody looking for Roscoe. And in the bed of this truck, parked way over by the road, was this mountain of a man. A giant. Know how some people are just larger? Eyes bigger. Their teeth. Their fingernails. Huge. Lying there, his knee was as big as my head. And he's passed out cold. So they dump a barrel of water over him. With the crowd all around, this man steps down off the tailgate and straps himself to this plow. Now, this is one of those big old farm plows. Heavy. Stuck in the ground where they'd left it half a year earlier. But he moved it. A little at first, then more. Steady. Slow. One giant step, then another. Face ready to blow like a steam whistle. And all these drunk farmers, these railroad men, coal diggers, wives, sisters, and cousins cheering and shouting. Two long rows on either side. Folks I'd never met before. All fixed on this man working like an animal. Pumping their effort in alongside him. Some moments I think you just swim into. The shouting. This blur of sound. And I realized that for the longest time I was staring across the crowd, past this man and his plow. It was right then my love appeared. Standing there. Right in front of me. I knew right away. Her hair the color of root beer, in this long dress that looked like it was made from a set of curtains. Turns out it was. Just like in that movie. But what really caught me was the way the sunlight shooting through the treetops picked out this little imperfection in her eye. This sparkling hunk of gold. I must have been thirty feet away, but I could see it as clear as a star.

Stiffly turning, Albert traces the path of the sun with the end of his cane.

Last spring, that young lady died in my arms, Albert says. It might seem odd, but that was her last request. For me to hold her. She was ill for so long. You know, you live for decades loving somebody, they're such a part of you. Can't sleep at night without them. Can't so much as plan your day. And sometimes you wonder, what's the point anyway. I miss her so. She said to me, I guess the world is done with me now. I guess it was. But I wasn't.

Between Albert and the Bus Driver now stands Albert's Wife in her homemade green dress. A quivering grin crosses her lips. She nods to the Bus Driver and imperceptibly wraps her fingers around Albert's hand resting on his cane.

I pray sometimes, Albert says. Kind of an old-fashioned idea. But I like it. Know what I pray for most?

What's that, the Bus Driver asks.

That there's a place where I will see her again, Albert says. Where more than her memory is a part of me again. But you want to know what else? The thing right after that?

What, the Bus Driver asks.

For one more day, Albert laughs. To not leave this place. Not quite yet, at least. To not lose my sense of how beautiful are the things around me. Because there are days when people drink beer in the sunshine. When the warm air melts the weight of their lives. When the light bounces off of the prettiest eyes you'll ever see and rips the heart right out of your chest. These things. I want these things. And I'm sure as hell not ready to give them up yet. Not yet.

With that, Albert carefully sloshes his way back across the field toward the waiting Passengers. She waves to him longingly and fades away. The Bus Driver's feet are stuck in the wet soil.

The closed sign still swings from the Paradise Diner's locked front door.

In the tiny storeroom, The Girl pulls a belt tight against The Boy's upper arm. A candle throws shadows across the food cans and buckets.

With cotton from a bottle of aspirin they found in the first-aid kit, she strains the drug into a needle from a soup spoon. Carefully, she squirts a bit of the liquid into the air.

Why did you do that, he asks.

Air bubbles, she says. Ready?

Guess so, he says, holding out a vein protruding from

the crook in his arm.

She slides the needle in. He winces. The Boy blinks, suddenly worried, as she pushes the mixture into his body.

He tries to speak. But a warm sensation spreads and he sinks into the floor. Eyes half closed. Mouth turning to a pronounced grin. The Girl repeats the steps for herself with the bag's second syringe.

Outside, Satan throws his hands into the air.

Then, as The Girl curls into a ball against the pickle barrels, her face grows flush. Her eyes watery and distant. Rolling onto her back, the drug soaks deeper and deeper into her smooth tissue. Her breath slows. Her heart stops.

Satan bursts through the diner's back door and into the storeroom. Knocking the candle across the concrete floor, he kneels beside her in the darkness, with long moans as she dies.

As he slowly tilts his face to the sky, tears fall from the well-worn corners of the Bus Driver's eyes.

You ready to keep moving, Albert calls.

Yeah, the Bus Driver says, making his way back toward the waiting crowd. Yeah, I'm ready.

FIFTEEN - THE TINKER'S DAMN

Not long after stepping off the bus, darkness all around him, Irv pushes through the engine block red front door of a bar they call the Tinker's Damn.

Somebody built this place out of a barn that kept the machines that cut the roads. Good spot for a quiet drink on the way from here to there.

They put it beside a truck brake. A big ditch piled with little rocks. The road twists by there before dipping into the next set of mountains. They build these gravel beds on big turns, to reach out and hold sixteen tons that lost its way. Safe and crumpled.

Irv steps through the doorway and looks around. Dim lightbulbs swing uncovered, low over the tables. Half-light disappears into the dark eaves of the barn. He walks over and leans his elbows on the bar top, so steady it might have grown there. Men in dirty coveralls line the walls, drinking and grumbling. Irv smiles. He's home.

The door opens and workers tumble in, exhausted. A half-dozen more finish their beers and shuffle out for night shifts. Stripping off his heavy coat, Irv looks up and stops. Hanging there above the bar is a genuine, vintage movie studio publicity photo of a once famous actress in a black-and-white red dress.

Irv's older brother Vernon stomps toward him with his hand out. Thin hips balancing a round middle. Leg turned with a limp.

Well, I'll be, Vernon says.

Irv pulls at Vernon, wrapping his arms around him. He looks Vernon in the eye and rubs his hand across his white hair.

Damn, Irv says. Look at you. Damn.

Got no business here, says their little brother, Ray, from across the room, shifting a broom handle in his hands like it's about to become a weapon.

These days their ages seem less far apart. But the differences are still clear as day. Vernon smiles at Irv and nods toward a table in the middle of the room.

Irv looks around. Bartender nowhere to be seen, he lays a couple bills on the bar, leaning across to find a bottle and glasses.

Get out, Ray says, widening his stance like a major leaguer.

Irv sits at Vernon's table, pouring.

Get out or I will throw you out, Ray growls through his teeth.

You look well, Vernon, says Irv.

I sure do, says Vernon.

How are you, Ray, Irv asks. You look like you want to sit down.

Screw you, Ray says.

Enough, barks Vernon. Enough!

Ray puts his hands on his hips and purses his lips the same way their Mother used to.

A long quiet swishes across the bar. Vernon and Irv stare into their whiskey. Ray stays like stone.

Irv decides to break the deadlock.

Vernon, I don't know if you noticed, but over there is a genuine movie studio photo of about the prettiest actress you'll ever see, he says.

Vernon cranes his neck.

No kidding, he says.

Irv watches Ray's eyes stubbornly shift to above the bar.

She was in this movie, Irv says. About raising horses in Indiana or something. Tell you the truth, I really don't remember. This was after you went to the Army. This movie showed at the Diamond downtown for a couple weeks, and I saw it about a hundred times. I mean, I never missed it. There was this actress in it, like I say. She was something else. So I offered the guy who owned the theater whatever nickels I had saved up for the picture they had of her hanging in the box office. Meant nothing to him, but I was just a kid. So no doing. I put it out of my mind. Then this one day. I wake up and there on the table is that very picture, in the frame and everything. Ray swiped it. Broke his arm climbing out the window of the place.

Irv smiles at Ray, looking for a reaction. Ray stares off, angry.

I left it behind, Irv says. Completely forgot about it until right this minute.

Ray uncrosses his arms and pours himself a drink.

You do have some nerve, he says.

Yeah, Irv says. How are you, Ray?

What do you mean, Ray asks.

Vernon wrote me, Irv says.

What about, Ray asks.

About how you're sick, Irv says.

I'm not sick, Ray says. He just wants us to talk.

Vernon chuckles. Ray collects dirty glasses from a nearby table and starts toward the bar.

Following a long gulp and a deep breath, Vernon leans in close to Irv. Irv leans closer. Vernon nods at Ray.

Hey, you know that guy, Vernon whispers as his eyes flash, angry. Seriously though, do you know that guy?

What do you mean, Irv asks.

That's the guy who stole my watch, Vernon says. I think he's wearing it right now.

Ray stands behind the bar, breaking up a block of ice. Irv walks over, confused.

Vernon, Irv says. He, uh . . .

Vernon's not all right in the head anymore, Irv, says Ray.

Comes and goes. Just something we live with.

Out from a curtain behind Ray, a small woman in an apron smiles toward them. Twirling a wash cloth, she puts her arm around Ray's thin waist, half his age and more familiar than Irv expected.

Hello, I'm Alice, she says.

This is Irv, says Ray.

Hello, Irv, she says.

Irv nods.

Do me a favor, Ray says. Take a lap. See who needs what.

Sure, Alice says, her hand sliding across the countertop.

So you work here, Irv asks.

Own it, Ray says. Last ten years.

No kidding, says Irv, nodding and looking around. Not bad at all.

No, not bad, Ray says.

Ray gathers up glasses from a stack behind the counter, polishes each one and sets them on another stack.

She reminds me of Carol, Irv says.

Yeah, Ray asks.

Yeah, Irv says.

Ray watches Alice.

Nah, I don't see it, he says.

How is she, Irv asks.

Who, Ray asks.

Carol, Irv says.

How would I know, Ray asks.

Irv jolts back a step.

What do you mean, Irv asks.

She left, Ray says. Long time ago. Just like you.

Why, Irv asks.

Ray stares across the barroom at Alice, then back at Irv.

Irv follows Ray's gaze.

Jesus, he says. How old is she?

Shut up, Irv, you don't know how it is, Ray says.

So explain it to me, Irv says, planting his fists on the bar, pissed in a way he doesn't like.

You shut up, Irv, Ray says.

Nah, Irv says. Nah. I think I need to understand this. What did you do? She catch you two, you and this barback? Your own Wife wasn't good enough?

It's not like that, Ray says.

Then how is it, Ray, Irv demands. Answer me. You idiot.

Ray looks up at Irv, raises a sparkling glass to the light and smashes it to the floor. He throws a towel over his shoulder and walks out from behind the bar. All over the room, heads turn back to their own business. Ray wipes tables. Irv follows him.

Answer me, Irv shouts, grabbing his shoulder. Ray shoves him hard.

I haven't seen you in thirty-eight years, Ray says. What do you know about it? What do you care? Things die slow, Irv. Some of us don't get to run away in the middle of the night. Maybe if you hadn't, you could have lent me your insight into the situation along the way. But you did, Irv. You left. So you got no right to tell me nothing.

Vernon stays still at the table, watching, waiting, staying out of it. Irv glares back at Ray. Caught in the headlights.

All I know is, you disappeared, Ray says. I mean, I know I wasn't paying much attention that weekend, since Carol and I'd talked ourselves into running off to get married over the state line. So wound up. So scared. Never would have gone if it wasn't for you. All talk, the both of us. We knew it. I remember how you gave us some money. Gave me your best suit. Wouldn't take no for an answer. Said, get going. No time like the present. So that's what we did. Just like you said. Always. And that was it. We weren't gone that long. What happened after that? It must've happened fast. Where'd you go?

Irv stares a hole through the floor.

It's complicated, he says. Things happen. Can't always expect a reason.

So they told me, Ray says. Said to leave it alone. Well, I say that's just not good enough. This town and its secrets. The feuds and fights. Vernon was grown and gone. You left me by myself here, right when I needed you. Without a word. Now, I know that happens. Wrong thing comes and catches up to a person and that's all there is to it. But whatever it was, you could have trusted me. You should have known that. Not supposed to be this way.

Irv says nothing. Ray stomps out of the bar. The rest of the room never cared less.

Vernon, I couldn't stay around to see them happy like that, Irv says. Rotten thing. No good for anybody. Better to take it on the road.

Yeah, says Vernon. I'd have done the same.

Irv finishes his drink.

I'll see you, Vern, he says.

Soon enough, Vernon says. Lord knows.

Irv walks over to the bar and puts on his coat. He looks over at Alice, warily staring back at him with the broom in her hands, cleaning up the broken glass. Irv smiles at her and puts his foot on a barstool rung. His knees creak and pop. His other foot lands hard on the bar. Irv reaches out and pulls the black and white photo from its place over the register. He studies the picture for a moment, wiping off a smudge on a corner of the tin-plated frame.

Irv climbs slowly off the bar and down to the floor, careful the whole way. He nods to Alice.

Don't think that's yours, she says, a shotgun now tucked under her arm.

The hell it ain't, Irv says, lets loose a laugh that ends with a tired sigh, and walks out of the Tinker's Damn with the picture his Brother gave him.

SIXTEEN - AND IN THE END

The bus now idles outside the depot it calls home. Switching the headlights off, finally, the Bus Driver runs all of his fingers up under his official blue hat and across his tired scalp. The remaining Passengers make their way to the asphalt and hustle off into the darkness. He glances back over the seat rows a last time. Resting against a window, the spun points of the an expensive wig shimmer in the dull light drifting in from outside. He smiles, walks back and jostles the snoring Widow's shoulder.

What's that, she asks, blearily.

End of the road, dear, he says.

Of course, she says. Help me up.

Taking her arm, he wobbles with her all the way down the bus steps.

I could use a cup of coffee, she moans, sleepy.

Leaning against the depot doorway, George waits for them.

Howdy, handsome, she says and stops, glancing back and forth, confused. Then she sees her wig still pressed against the bus window.

Ma'am, George says.

This is George, the Bus Driver says. Stick with him and he'll get you what you need.

Behind George, next to the empty terminal, a wide, plain door without any sort of support appears and swings open. A comfortable puddle of light falls across the woman's face.

Everything's alright now, the Bus Driver says.

She hugs him. George takes her hand and walks her gently toward the door. Suddenly, she stops and grabs the Bus Driver's sleeve.

You know, I haven't been very good, she says.

Hey, the Bus Driver says. A-plus for effort.

George and the Bus Driver watch her go.

Can you imagine, the Bus Driver says. Knowing what you know. What it would be like to really rest, never realizing a million flips of a million coins all over the world are stopping hearts and bending trees to the ground? To feel, somehow, that someone else is driving. So you can completely close your eyes a bit. Falling backwards with your arms out. Never hitting the ground.

A little, George says.

So here's the plan, the Bus Driver says. Keep an eye on things for me. Don't worry, the whole rig runs itself.

He gives George a reassuring nod as he walks away.

Where are you going now, George asks.

To bed, the Bus Driver says.

The Bus Driver finds Jack Eddy sitting on the curb around the corner. In the glow of the parking lot lights, he scribbles at his notepad, eyebrows twisted.

Make sure to carry the one, the Bus Driver chimes.

No kidding, Eddy laughs.

Well, I'll tell you something, the Bus Driver says. You've got a clever way of looking at things, if you ask me. I like it. Tell people. They'll listen.

In not too long, the Bus Driver trudges down a short row of rotting wooden shacks leaning over a path in bright moonlight. Feet fighting gravity in turn.

He slumps inside the door of a small, square house and peels off his boots. Socks gone, he leans back against the wall, stretching grateful toes.

His mind fades from this body, which he pours onto an unsteady wooden chair. He reaches over to yank the cord on a second-hand floor lamp. The filament sputters. Thin shadows filter over a dusty table and neatly made bed.

Reaching above himself, he pulls a can of tuna off a shelf

and sets it on the table. Staring down at the fat, blue fish on the front, he spots the opener all the way on the other side of the little room. Pressing thumbs into his eyes, his shirt hits the floor. He falls heavy onto the thin mattress.

The lumps mold to his crumpled body. Holding his hands in front of his face, admiring their design, smelling his own sweat rising over the bed, he hears a mouse scurry behind the wall.

The bulb fuzzes to itself and calmly burns out. The Bus Driver lifts his head and laughs as his eyes adjust to moonbeams sticking to the wall. Then, for the very first time, he slips happily into sleep.

Thanks For Reading!
More Info:
AdamFike.com
Goodreads.com